Lynda Hall
Editor

D1569953

Lesbian Self-Writing: The Embodiment of Experience

Lesbian Self-Writing: The Embodiment of Experience has been co-published simultaneously as *Journal of Lesbian Studies,* Volume 4, Number 4 2000.

Pre-publication
REVIEWS,
COMMENTARIES,
EVALUATIONS . . .

"***L****esbian Self-Writing* probes the intersection of love for words and love for women, asserting that lesbians inhabit language 'with a difference.' In writing that is a times luminous and erotic and is always evocative, the writers of this volume explore how much personal risk lies in the writing life."

Beverly Burch, PhD
Psychotherapist and author of Other Women: Lesbian/Bisexual Experience and Psychoanalytic Views of Women *and* On Intimate Terms: The Psychology of Difference in Lesbian Relationships

More pre-publication
REVIEWS, COMMENTARIES, EVALUATIONS . . .

"**L**ynda Hall is eminently qualified to create a book of reflections on lesbian autobiography by an impressive group of writers from the U.S. and Canada. Her thoughtful introduction incorporates both feminist analysis and postmodern discourse. The seventeen pieces are readable and personal, offering a rare glimpse into the complex writing process for giants of lesbian letters like Kate Millett, Nicole Brossard, and Karla Jay; popular authors like Jewelle Gomez, Ruthann Robson, and Lesléa Newman; and newer writers like Mary Cappello and Anna Livia.

I wish all my community college writing students could absorb *Lesbian Self-Writing*. Each piece testifies eloquently to the importance of writing the truth of one's life as an act of self-realization, healing, and empowerment not only for people marginalized by their race, class, or sexual orientation, but for anyone who has experienced pain and trauma. This is a fine book and a pleasure to read."

Nancy Manahan, PhD
English Department, Minneapolis Community and Technical College; author of Lesbian Nuns:
Breaking Silence *and* On My Honor:
Lesbians Reflect on Their
Scouting Experience

"**A** rich collection of autobiographical accounts by lesbian writers and visual artists addressing their personal and complex networks of creativity: desire, memory, politics, parenting, and the agency of artistic and literary production. Without making claims for a lesbian aesthetic per se, the essays develop a compelling case for the place of sexuality in lives devoted to social transformation and community building–through such acts as writing, giving public readings, and teaching."

Leigh Gilmore
*Associate Professor of English
Ohio State University;
Author of* Autobiographics:
A Feminist Theory
of Women's Self-Representation
and Co-Editor of Autobiography
and Postmodernism

Lesbian Self-Writing: The Embodiment of Experience

Lesbian Self-Writing: The Embodiment of Experience has been co-published simultaneously as *Journal of Lesbian Studies,* Volume 4, Number 4 2000.

The *Journal of Lesbian Studies* Monographic "Separates"

Below is a list of "separates," which in serials librarianship means a special issue simultaneously published as a special journal issue or double-issue *and* as a "separate" hardbound monograph. (This is a format which we also call a "DocuSerial.")

"Separates" are published because specialized libraries or professionals may wish to purchase a specific thematic issue by itself in a format which can be separately cataloged and shelved, as opposed to purchasing the journal on an on-going basis. Faculty members may also more easily consider a "separate" for classroom adoption.

"Separates" are carefully classified separately with the major book jobbers so that the journal tie-in can be noted on new book order slips to avoid duplicate purchasing.

You may wish to visit Haworth's website at . . .

http://www.HaworthPress.com

. . . to search our online catalog for complete tables of contents of these separates and related publications.

You may also call 1-800-HAWORTH (outside US/Canada: 607-722-5857), or Fax 1-800-895-0582 (outside US/Canada: 607-771-0012), or e-mail at:

getinfo@haworthpressinc.com

Lesbian Self-Writing: The Embodiment of Experience, edited by Lynda Hall (Vol. 4, No. 4, 2000). *"Probes the intersection of love for words and love for women. . . . Luminous, erotic, evocative." (Beverly Burch, PhD, psychotherapist and author,* Other Women: Lesbian/Bisexual Experience and Psychoanalytic Views of Women *and* On Intimate Terms: The Psychology of Difference in Lesbian Relationships)

'Romancing the Margins'? Lesbian Writing in the 1990s, edited by Gabriele Griffin, PhD (Vol. 4, No. 2, 2000). *Explores lesbian issues through the mediums of books, movies, and poetry and offers readers critical essays that examine current lesbian writing and discuss how recent movements have tried to remove racist and anti-gay themes from literature and movies.*

From Nowhere to Everywhere: Lesbian Geographies, edited by Gill Valentine, PhD (Vol. 4, No. 1, 2000). *"A significant and worthy contribution to the ever growing literature on sexuality and space. . . . A politically significant volume representing the first major collection on lesbian geographies. . . . I will make extensive use of this book in my courses on social and cultural geography and sexuality and space." (Jon Binnie, PhD, Lecturer in Human Geography, Liverpool, John Moores University, United Kingdom)*

Lesbians, Levis and Lipstick: The Meaning of Beauty in Our Lives, edited by Jeanine C. Cogan, PhD, and Joanie M. Erickson (Vol. 3, No. 4, 1999). *Explores lesbian beauty norms and the effects these norms have on lesbian women.*

Lesbian Sex Scandals: Sexual Practices, Identities, and Politics, edited by Dawn Atkins, MA (Vol. 3, No. 3, 1999). *"Grounded in material practices, this collection explores confrontation and coincidence among identity politics, 'scandalous' sexual practices, and queer theory and feminism. . . . It expands notions of lesbian identification and lesbian community." (Maria Pramaggiore, PhD, Assistant Professor, Film Studies, North Carolina State University, Raleigh)*

The Lesbian Polyamory Reader: Open Relationships, Non-Monogamy, and Casual Sex, edited by Marcia Munson and Judith P. Stelboum, PhD (Vol. 3, No. 1/2, 1999). *"Offers reasonable, logical, and persuasive explanations for a style of life I had not seriously considered before. . . . A terrific read." (Beverly Todd, Acquisitions Librarian, Estes Park Public Library, Estes Park, Colorado)*

Living "Difference": Lesbian Perspectives on Work and Family Life, edited by Gillian A. Dunne, PhD (Vol. 2, No. 4, 1998). *"A fascinating, groundbreaking collection. . . . Students and professionals in psychiatry, psychology, sociology, and anthropology will find this work extremely useful and thought provoking."* (Nanette K. Gartrell, MD, Associate Clinical Professor of Psychiatry, University of California at San Francisco Medical School)

Acts of Passion: Sexuality, Gender, and Performance, edited by Nina Rapi, MA, and Maya Chowdhry, MA (Vol. 2, No. 2/3, 1998). *"This significant and impressive publication draws together a diversity of positions, practices, and polemics in relation to postmodern lesbian performance and puts them firmly on the contemporary cultural map."* (Lois Keidan, Director of Live Arts, Institute of Contemporary Arts, London, United Kingdom)

Gateways to Improving Lesbian Health and Health Care: Opening Doors, edited by Christy M. Ponticelli, PhD (Vol. 2, No. 1, 1997). *"An unprecedented collection that goes to the source for powerful and poignant information on the state of lesbian health care."* (Jocelyn C. White, MD, Assistant Professor of Medicine, Oregon Health Sciences University; Faculty, Portland Program in General Internal Medicine, Legacy Portland Hospitals, Portland, Oregon)

Classics in Lesbian Studies, edited by Esther Rothblum, PhD (Vol. 1, No. 1, 1996). *"Brings together a collection of powerful chapters that cross disciplines and offer a broad vision of lesbian lives across race, age, and community."* (Michele J. Eliason, PhD, Associate Professor, College of Nursing, The University of Iowa)

YOU FEEL PAIN SO
DEEPLY
BECAUSE YOU CAN
DESCRIBE IT SO WELL

Lesbian Self-Writing: The Embodiment of Experience

Lynda Hall
Editor

Lesbian Self-Writing: The Embodiment of Experience has been co-published simultaneously as *Journal of Lesbian Studies,* Volume 4, Number 4 2000.

Harrington Park Press
An Imprint of
The Haworth Press, Inc.
New York • London • Oxford

Published by

Harrington Park Press®, 10 Alice Street, Binghamton, NY 13904-1580 USA

Harrington Park Press® is an imprint of The Haworth Press, Inc., 10 Alice Street, Binghamton, NY 13904-1580 USA.

Lesbian Self-Writing: The Embodiment of Experience has been co-published simultaneously as *Journal of Lesbian Studies,* Volume 4, Number 4 2000.

The development, preparation, and publication of this work has been undertaken with great care. However, the publisher, employees, editors, and agents of The Haworth Press and all imprints of The Haworth Press, Inc., including The Haworth Medical Press® and Pharmaceutical Products Press®, are not responsible for any errors contained herein or for consequences that may ensue from use of materials or information contained in this work. Opinions expressed by the author(s) are not necessarily those of The Haworth Press, Inc.

Cover artwork by Shani Mootoo.
Cover design by Marylouise Doyle.

Library of Congress Cataloging-in-Publication Data

Lesbian self-writing : the embodiment of experience / Lynda Hall, editor.
     p. cm.
    Includes bibliographical references and index.
    ISBN 1-56023-143-2 (alk. paper)–ISBN 1-56023-144-0 (alk. paper)
    1. Lesbians' writings, American–History and criticism. 2. Women authors, American–Biography–History and criticism. 3. Women authors, Canadian–Biography–History and criticism. 4. Lesbians' writings, Canadian–History and criticism. 5. Lesbians–Biography–History and criticism. 6. Autobiography–Women authors. 7. Lesbians in literature. I. Hall, Lynda.
PS153.L46 L458 2000
810.9′9206643–dc21
                                                           00-061339

INDEXING & ABSTRACTING

Contributions to this publication are selectively indexed or abstracted in print, electronic, online, or CD-ROM version(s) of the reference tools and information services listed below. This list is current as of the copyright date of this publication. See the end of this section for additional notes.

- *Abstracts in Social Gerontology: Current Literature on Aging*

- *BUBL Information Service, an Internet-based Information Service for the UK higher education community <URL: http//bubl.ac.uk/>*

- *CNPIEC Reference Guide: Chinese National Directory of Foreign Periodicals*

- *Contemporary Women's Issues*

- *Feminist Periodicals: A Current Listing of Contents*

- *FINDEX, free Internet directory of over 150,000 publications from around the world <www.publist.com>*

- *Gay & Lesbian Abstracts*

- *GenderWatch <www.slinfocom>*

- *HOMODOK/"Relevant" Bibliographic database, Documentation Centre for Gay & Lesbian Studies, University of Amsterdam (selective printed abstracts in "Homologie" and bibliographic computer databases covering cultural, historical, social and political aspects of gay & lesbian topics)*

- *IGLSS Abstracts <http://www.iglss.org>*

- *Index to Periodical Articles Related to Law*

- *OCLC Public Affairs Information Service <www.pais.org>*

(continued)

- *Referativnyi Zhurnal (Abstracts Journal of the All-Russian Institute of Scientific and Technical Information)*

- *Social Services Abstracts <http://www.csa.com>*

- *Sociological Abstracts (SA) <http://www.csa.com>*

- *Studies on Women Abstracts*

- *Women's Studies Index (indexed comprehensively)*

Special Bibliographic Notes related to special journal issues (separates) and indexing/abstracting:

- indexing/abstracting services in this list will also cover material in any "separate" that is co-published simultaneously with Haworth's special thematic journal issue or DocuSerial. Indexing/abstracting usually covers material at the article/chapter level.
- monographic co-editions are intended for either non-subscribers or libraries which intend to purchase a second copy for their circulating collections.
- monographic co-editions are reported to all jobbers/wholesalers/approval plans. The source journal is listed as the "series" to assist the prevention of duplicate purchasing in the same manner utilized for books-in-series.
- to facilitate user/access services all indexing/abstracting services are encouraged to utilize the co-indexing entry note indicated at the bottom of the first page of each article/chapter/contribution.
- this is intended to assist a library user of any reference tool (whether print, electronic, online, or CD-ROM) to locate the monographic version if the library has purchased this version but not a subscription to the source journal.
- individual articles/chapters in any Haworth publication are also available through the Haworth Document Delivery Service (HDDS).

Lesbian Self-Writing:
The Embodiment of Experience

CONTENTS

ABOUT THE EDITOR

Lynda Hall, a sessional instructor at the University of Calgary, graduated with her PhD in English in 1998. Her teaching and research focus on lesbian autobiographical writing, the performativity of gender, and cultural representations of lesbian bodies and lesbian lives. She has published widely in various journals, including *Callaloo: A Journal of African-American and African Arts and Letters*; *Sex Roles*; *Ariel: A Review of International English Literature*; *Canadian Theatre Review*; *Tessera*; *Journal of Dramatic Theory and Criticism*; *Postmodern Culture*; *Canadian Literature*; *Women's Studies International*; and *Journal of Gay, Lesbian, and Bisexual Identity*. Hall has essays forthcoming in 2000 in *A/B: Auto/Biographical Studies*, a special issue–"Queer Autobiographies," and *This Bridge Called My Back–Twenty Years Later* (edited by Gloria Anzaldúa and AnaLouise Keating). Hall edited, completed the introductory essay, and contributed a paper to a special issue of the *International Journal of Sexuality and Gender Studies* (volume 5.2, 2000), which is entitled *Converging Terrains: Gender, Body, Environment and Technology*. Address correspondence to Lynda Hall, Department of English, University of Calgary, 2500 University Drive N.W., Calgary, Alberta, Canada T2N 1N4.

Acknowledgments

First and foremost, I would like to thank the seventeen lesbian writers who have generously offered their time and creative efforts to this project. In these essays they share their diversity of experiences and perspectives and passionately illustrate the richness of "telling" through self-writing. Thank you all. The second acknowledgment is to my professors at the University of Calgary; each in their own areas of scholarship provided solid foundations for my current scholarly endeavours–Susan Bennett, Susan Stratton, Susan Rudy, and Jeanne Perreault. I wish to extend my special thanks to Jeanne Perreault, who has been an ongoing source of inspiration, strength, and intellectual excitement since my undergraduate years, and whose *Writing Selves: Contemporary Feminist Autography* provides the theoretical grounding for this project. I am extremely grateful to the following for their encouragement, friendship, and insightful comments on the project and on drafts of the introduction: Susan Paulson, Marie Lovrod, Karla Jay, Mary Meigs, Betsy Warland, Analouise Keating, and Mary Cappello. Finally, thank you to Kathy, for sharing the precious moments of this life's journey, and for continually nurturing my imagination and my spirit.

Grateful acknowledgement is made to the following sources for allowing me to reprint material:

Excerpts from *A.D., A Memoir,* © 1995 by Kate Millett, are reprinted by permission of the author, Kate Millett, and by permission of W.W. Norton & Company.

"Writing Life" from *Writing as Witness: Essay and Talk* by Beth Brant is reprinted by permission of the author.

From *Collected Poems* by Frank O'Hara, Copyright © 1969 by Maureen Granville-Smith, Administratix of the Estate of Frank O'Hara. Reprinted by permission of Alfred A. Knopf Inc.

Introduction: Lesbians Loving Wor(l)ds: Communicating Acts

Lynda Hall

KEYWORDS. Lesbians, self-writing, body, language, memory

> What lives on will come back to inscribe its yes, a proud yes amid energy and anguish, at the heart of that which never changes inside of us for, as we know, the body never forgets that other very ancient body which obliges us to sign our very brief story in history. (Brossard, *Contemporary Authors,* 39)

Lynda Hall, a sessional instructor at the University of Calgary, graduated with her PhD in English in 1998. Her teaching and research focus on lesbian autobiographical writing, the performativity of gender, and cultural representations of lesbian bodies and lesbian lives. She has published widely in various journals, including *Sex Roles*; *Ariel: A Review of International English Literature*; *Canadian Theatre Review*; *Tessera*; *Journal of Dramatic Theory and Criticism*; *Postmodern Culture*; *Canadian Literature*; *Women's Studies International*; and *Journal of Gay, Lesbian, and Bisexual Identity.* Hall has essays forthcoming in 2000 *in A/B: Auto/Biographical Studies,* a special issue–"Queer Autobiographies"; *Callalloo,* a special issue–"Plum Nelly: New Essays on African American Queer Studies"; and *This Bridge Called My Back–Twenty Years Later* (edited by Gloria Anzaldúa and AnaLouise Keating). She edited, completed the introductory essay, and contributed a paper to a special issue of the *International Journal of Sexuality and Gender Studies* (volume 5.2, 2000), which is entitled *Converging Terrains: Gender, Body, Environment and Technology.*

Address correspondence to: Lynda Hall, Department of English, University of Calgary, 2500 University Drive N.W., Calgary, Alberta, Canada T2N 1N4.

[Haworth co-indexing entry note]: "Introduction: Lesbians Loving Wor(l)ds: Communicating Acts." Hall, Lynda. Co-published simultaneously in *Journal of Lesbian Studies* (Harrington Park Press, an imprint of The Haworth Press, Inc.) Vol. 4, No. 4, 2000, pp. 1-19; and: *Lesbian Self-Writing: The Embodiment of Experience* (ed: Lynda Hall) Harrington Park Press, an imprint of The Haworth Press, Inc., 2000, pp. 1-19. Single or multiple copies of this article are available for a fee from The Haworth Document Delivery Service [1-800-342-9678, 9:00 a.m. - 5:00 p.m. (EST). E-mail address: getinfo@haworthpressinc.com].

Lynda Hall
Photo by Kathy Koole. Used by permission.

Many contemporary lesbian artists passionately resist silencing through the empowering act of self-writing. Pivoting around issues of identity, their writings embody a nuanced celebration of survival and a recuperation of lesbian desires and experiences. At the same time, textual enactments of selves-in-process offer coping and survival strategies for others to adopt. Works by lesbian writers reject the silences surrounding the cumulative repressive forces that impact their lives- silences that perpetuate the patriarchal, heterosexual status quo. Foregrounding the connections between lesbian sexuality and textuality, lesbian writers overcome isolation by sharing their experiences and providing community. Bringing the voices together into a "chorus" facilitates self-understanding for the writer through the writing process, for the lesbian reader who may find witness and expression to her own past (and/or present) experience, and for the heterosexual reader who may contemplate heretofore unconsidered aspects of "other's" lives. The counter-discourse provided through testimonial writings by many lesbian writers constitutes a powerful challenge to social oppression. Converging as a community through writing, they resist putative labels such as "outsider," while in some circumstances the label is embraced. Lesbian identities that are invisible on the surface of the body become "real" through the self-written word. Nicole Brossard links the writing "act" with creating reality: "we give birth to ourselves in the world. Only through literally creating ourselves in the world do we declare our existence and from there make our presences known in the order of the real and the symbolic" (*Aerial Letter* 134).

In this edited collection I bring together papers that focus on lesbian self-writing where memory, language, body, experience, and deliberations on the "practice" and "process" of writing converge. In the fall of 1998, I invited papers from writers whose works I have long admired and who clearly identify the crucial role self-writing plays in their lives. The enthusiastic response I received from the writers testifies to the relevance of this project. The writers included in this collection are: Maya Chowdhry, Nicole Brossard, Beth Brant, Karla Jay, Mary Meigs, Mary Cappello, Kate Millett, Shani Mootoo, Jane Rule, Betsy Warland, Vanessa Scrivens, Jess Wells, Ruthann Robson, Lesléa Newman, Anna Livia, Jewelle Gomez and Mary Wings. The writers' meditations on the genesis of writing, with reference to past, new and/or forthcoming works, provide unique perspectives. Embodying the boundary-crossings enacted in their lives, their works span diverse genres; they often include many modes of writing within one paper, such as autobiographical prose, poetry, fiction-theory, dream analysis, letter, drama script, artwork, and interview. The strong urge to create takes varied forms. Several of the contributors are also visual artists, performance artists, teachers, and editors, and this multifaceted dynamic of creative activity provides a complex perspective on the lives lived. Shani Mootoo's artwork appears on the cover of this collection.

Lesbian Self-Writing: The Embodiment of Experience draws together self-reflective writing into conversations precipitated by frequent thematic intersections. The authors celebrate pleasures in life and also they enunciate the tensions and problematic experiences that interweave through many lives. Their writerly witness to subversive acts of gender and sexuality boundary-crossings provides alternative choices for others. In frank words, they expose the cultural anxieties constituted by open interrogation of and threat to the heterosexual, male ideological hegemony. Painful issues engaged include childhood sexual abuse, rape, family rejection due to homosexual tendencies, health difficulties, psychological problems (related to homosexuality, gender disidentification, physical looks, loss [love/death], racism, exile [home/country]), and legal issues (child custody, health problems and partner access, inheritance, immigration, discrimination in the workplace and housing environment). Testimonies to rights that have been gained over the years provide an enabling history of the consequences of "speaking out" and demanding that oppressions are not silenced and thereby perpetuated.

A common theme is the pain experienced when growing up in a family that does not accept an individual's feelings and sexual desires, followed by the later deliberations on early adulthood or middle life and the struggles to become acceptable to parental figures and society in general. Those individuals who do not conform to heterosexual imperatives often experience charges of "madness" or insanity. Writing the self is one strategy employed to counter these charges and to insist upon one's own reality. Gloria Anzaldúa acknowledges, "I, for one, define my life and construct my identities through the process of reading and writing" ("To(o) Queer the Writer" 257). The autobiographical impulse often is generated by the desire to cope with the splitting forced upon the mind and body by homophobic marginalization, and the wish to make visible the injustices suffered. Many of the writers deliberate the loss of love in a world where that love is made difficult to achieve. Writers who address their refusal to accept sexual policing and disciplining make visible more open attitudes towards sexuality and acceptance of freer modes of behaviour. The experiences written and thus witnessed may facilitate others' understanding of their past or present experiences. The moments of lives shared may provide information for experiences that are imminent in the future, such as preparing for the birth of a child, facing the death of a loved one, or dealing with aging.

This collection follows in a tradition of previous works that include lesbian explorations of the self through writing, such as *This Bridge Called My Back: Writings by Radical Women of Color,* edited by Gloria Anzaldúa and Cherríe Moraga (1981, 1983); *InVersions: Writings by Dykes, Queers & Lesbians,* edited by Betsy Warland (1991); *A*

Gathering of Spirit, edited by Beth Brant (1988); and the more recently published volumes *Dyke Life: A Celebration of the Lesbian Experience,* edited by Karla Jay (1995), and *butch/femme: Inside Lesbian Gender,* edited by Sally Munt (1998)–volumes infused with intimate, personal, embodied reflections on gender and sexuality.

In this introductory essay I deliberately avoid any comment on the specific writings included in this collection. Instead, I prefer to allow the writers' words to speak for themselves and I hope that readers will explore each of the unique perspectives offered. The writers' explorations of the genesis of writing encourage further inquiry into the imbrication of autobiographical writing, imagination, self, identity, and the body. The following discussion of key themes and practices draws upon works by the most significant lesbian writers who engage self-writing in our time. While the issues are complex and inextricable, the trajectory of this engagement flows through investigations of language, the "process" of writing, self-discovery through writing, the healing potential of writing, the risks involved in writing, desires to create community, and finally, an urgent encouragement to others to write their experiences as well.

Writing about personal experiences breaks the pervasive silencing of lesbian lives. The "telling" possibilities are complex, including witnessing and exposing the most personal and the most crucial events. Reflecting on her life after being forced to become aware of her own mortality, Audre Lorde writes, "what I most regretted were my silences. . . . My silences had not protected me. Your silence will not protect you" (*Cancer Journals* 20). Direct address to the reader as "you" opens a space of dialogue. Lorde articulates the role that writing plays in piecing together her past and providing a means to re-order the past in the present: "This is an important function of the telling of experience. I am also writing to sort out for myself who I was and was becoming throughout that time" (53), she explains. It is informative to compare the changes over time in terms of lesbians' ability to "name" the self; in particular, the discrepancy between the freedoms articulated by some contemporary writers in comparison to the difficulties still experienced by others indicates that voice and determined visibility are still necessary political strategies. In *Flying* (1974), Kate Millett shares a "telling" conversation that she had with Doris Lessing about her struggles with silencing forces, and the need to fight back against intimidation; Millett recalls "feeling so vulnerable, my god, a Lesbian. Sure, an experience of human beings. But not described. Not permitted. It has no traditions. No language. No history of agreed values." "But of course people wish to know," [Lessing] interrupts. "And you cannot be intimidated into silence. Or the silence is prolonged forever." (444)

Breaking silences often occurs through an embrace of the beauty of language and its communication possibilities. The writers' joy in a "play" with words enhances the powerful "acts" of expressing the self. The indispensably sensuous nature of words, the erotics of language, is a major theme. Mary Cappello's first words in Chapter One of *Night Bloom: A Memoir* express the spiralling desire of and for language. She writes, "Snapdragons, if you press the hairy underside of their throats ever so gently, will speak. As a child, I wanted to eat every blossom in my father's garden, until I learned the pleasure in my mouth of their names: calla lily, cosmos, rose eclipse, dahlia" (3). In a writerly journey down the "garden path" in the mind, Cappello links memories of her mother with creativity and peace:

I see my mother from all sides through the tunnel of memory's lens. My mother is still. My mother is clear. My mother is clearly quiescent. And even though the feeling is liquid, my mother does not dissolve in this memory of the garden so much as she resolves, is resolved, finds momentary resolution in the shade of a cherry tree or as she bends to break a sprig of parsley or, buoyed up by a trail of roses by her side, looks up to the sky. (5)

"Witnessing" is a word that recurs in Cappello's *Night Bloom*; witnessing the beauty and mystery of the blooming Cereus plant parallels the writing and witnessing of life-in-process. The end of *Night Bloom* circles back to the beginning; Cappello recalls that "my mother would stay in the backyard for hours. Studying. Wondering. Writing. Celebrating. Witnessing" (250). Cappello's observation that "I came to think of the [Cereus] plant both as something we need witness and something that might witness us" (251) links the sensuous acts of writing with desires to "see" and "be seen"–for the self to understand and to be understood. Noting "How long I sit at my writing desk composing myself, composing my family" (249), she articulates the role that writing plays in re-creating the self and the family; through sensuous language, a sense of composure and reconciliation with the past is attempted. The notion of "composing" the self also acknowledges the performativity and active agency involved in the "process" of writing the self. The personal stories of joy and pain that spiral through *Night Bloom: A Memoir* echo in the dramatic unfolding of Cereus blooms in Shani Mootoo's *Cereus Blooms at Night* and, as well, in Cappello's comment on Dr. Kate Bornstein's use of "that eccentric phrase–'family plant'" (243) to describe the blooming of meaning across generations. "Looking back" retrospectively on her writing from twenty years ago, Cappello acknowledges the "opportunity I had taken all my life to use language–that most flimsy, unpredictable, unreliable of substances–to hold something close" (124).

"Telling" stories hold memories "close" for many lesbian writers. Demonstrating the sensuous connections of the body, language, memory, and desire, Betsy Warland's collection of poetry *What Holds Us Here* celebrates "how seductive story is" (43); with reference to the interior of the body and the spiritual, psychological, and intellectual darkness of unknowingness, Warland delves into "the body / the dark continent / so familiar, so / unknowable, its / language / two skins / touching" (126-127). Warland celebrates "touching" words and the ability to hold another "close" through language and through love. In her poem "wildrose buds," the seductively petalled voices resound: "expectant pink of wildrose buds taunt me most their sepals' / sensuous-green-adagio to warmth, slow-motion-desire exquisite / anticipation of the in-between / how your lips swell and part beneath the heat of my breath" (139).

As well as celebrating the pleasures of language, the writers explore the complex ways language structures the world around us in terms of power dynamics. They expose the "violence of rhetoric" that Teresa de Lauretis identifies (*Technologies of Gender* 34) as it impacts upon lesbian lives. The series of poems that form Warland's *"In A Word"* illustrate the possibility for words to separate the writer from the experience; she writes, "only details distinguish us / often details extinguish us / 'now, words and ideas will always slip themselves / between me and the feeling,' / us and / others" (*What Holds Us Here* 44-45). Memories and verb tense reveal levels of meaning and expose the self-in-process through time: "past tense = present tense = future tense = / a / tense situation" (45), Warland writes. As Warland's poem illustrates, the writers in this collection demonstrate the desire and the power in recuperating memories and selves across time through language.

Gender dynamics in linguistic forms are also a topic frequently examined in lesbian writings. Language structures our world, and "holds us here," as Warland suggests, but awareness of this constituting process and its impact on self-identity promotes conscious manipulation of language's bountiful possibilities for communicating "other"-wise. For instance, Anna Livia's book *Pronoun Envy* explores the use feminist novelists have made of invented non-gendered pronouns as a way of avoiding the generic masculine and thus, in the process, promoting gender equality and naming the self.

Self-naming is a crucial act of agency. Cross-genre work mirrors the boundary-crossings of gender and sexuality that many of these lesbian writers perform. Nicole Brossard's seductive *She Would Be the First Sentence of My Next Novel* (Mercury, 1999) embodies in content and form a resistance to rigid categories of genre, sexuality, gender, and singular self. English and French text appear in side-by-side dialogue. The volume is an extended meditation on the writing process–the "act" itself–and a celebration of the imbrication of lesbian sexual and textual desire, of the poetic and the erotic. Mary Cappello's *Night Bloom: A Memoir* similarly exemplifies the rich possibilities in crossing genres; her personal record interweaves diverse forms, including the bi-lingual journals of her Italian grandfather, Sicilian folklore, dreamwork, and her mother's poetry. She demonstrates the inextricability of the public and the private by including quotations from such writers as Rainer Maria Rilke and from newspaper articles.

Self-writing is a vital process that allows individuals to express their realities and their hoped-for dreams and desires. Words move the imagination. Self-writing is frequently a transformational act of self-discovery and self-exploration. Nicole Brossard writes, "Between the individual and the writer there is a free space, a mysterious landscape where one discovers and dares things that the individual cannot afford. It is in that space that I learn about myself and can transform myself" ("Interview" 189). Often, self-writing constitutes a celebration of life and survival, and offers a powerful avenue to self-invention, self-re-creation, and self-affirmation for those who suffer oppression at the intersections of gender, sex, sexuality, race, and class differences. With poignancy and power many lesbian artists transform pain into a celebration of life that every woman can use. Articulating their individual, embodied experiences, they take agency and refuse reduction, over-simplification, and/or doubt about the truth of their memories. Assuming the authority to define their experiences is an act of agency. Lesbian writers often highlight the potential positive influence writings have, both through providing witness and testimony for others to identify with (as demonstrated above by the words from Mary Cappello's *Night Bloom*), and through encouraging social transformation. Writing in order to promote change is a powerful act. Beth Brant asks, "What good is this pen, this yellow paper, if I can't fashion them into tools or weapons to change our lives?" (*Food & Spirits* 14).

Further, self-writing often includes the use of imagination to create things differently. Kate Millett suggests that writing "is a way of inventing the self. Striving toward one you can live with" (*Flying* 640). Impossible situations can be re-invented and re-visited, perhaps resulting in reconciliation of difficult relationships. The possibility to envision another way of being opens up alternatives. Daphne Marlatt relates writing the self and exploring identity to the social environment that impacts selfhood; she states, "It is exactly at the confluence of fiction (the self or selves we might be) and analysis (of the roles we have found ourselves in, defined in a complex socio-familial weave), it is in the confluence of the two that autobiography occurs, the self writing its way to life, whole life" ("Self-Representation" 15).

A significant subject in this collection is the actual act–the "process"–of writing the self. Nicole Brossard notes, "one might ask where do we draw the line between the individual's life, the fiction and the writing . . . though personal events can transform my writing, it is not the story of my life but the story of the creative process which is interesting" ("Interview" 188). Her words embody the "autography" that Jeanne Perreault identifies. Perreault suggests that "One way in which autography differs from autobiography is that it is not necessarily concerned with the process or unfolding of life events, but rather makes the writing itself an aspect of the selfhood the writer experiences and brings into being" (*Writing Selves: Contemporary Feminist Autography* 3-4). Describing the significance of the "process" of self-writing to her sense of selfhood, Kate Millett speaks of "Writing to find out who I am . . . a bridge between the voice talking in my head and prose as I'd known it. It was to explain myself to myself" (*Flying* 101).

Also exemplifying Jeanne Perreault's discussion on bringing the self into being through the writing "process," Gloria Anzaldúa names the crucial role that writing performs in her life. She acknowledges, "the world I create in the writing compensates for what the real world does not give me. By writing I put order in the world, give it a handle, so I can grasp it. . . . I write to record what others erase when I speak, to rewrite the stories others have miswritten about me, about you" ("Speaking In Tongues" 169). Self-writing provides the opportunity to create order out of disorder, and to create presence instead of absences and silence. She continues by acknowledging that she writes "To become more intimate with myself and you. To discover myself, to preserve myself, to make myself. . . . I will write about the unmentionables, never mind the outraged gasp of the censor and the audience" ("Speaking In Tongues" 169). Discovering the self through writing is a long and complex journey that many lesbian writers describe, in all of its pain and pleasures along the way. Many lesbian writers describe the strategic necessity to articulate often-silenced experiences, and the difficulty, but necessity, to resist the impulse to give in to powerful forces of censorship

Jeanne Perreault suggests that in "autography" the "writers make 'I' and 'we' signify both continuity with an ongoing life in a body and a community, and dissociation within that life–gaps, amputations, silences" (4). "Dissociation" and dislocation are words that frequently recur within the lines of lesbian self-writings. In *The Cancer Journals,* Audre Lorde reflects on the potential of writing "acts" to overcome "dissociation"; she explains, "I was always listening to a concert of voices from inside myself. . . . all I had to do was remember the pieces and put them together" (31). The "act" of gathering pieces together, and Perreault's analysis of "autography" as a process that highlights the imbrication of the self, textuality, and community, are further exemplified by Beth Brant. In *Writing as Witness,* Brant claims, "it is a truth that writing put me on a path towards freedom. I don't mean personal freedom. I mean freedom to be a loving and useful member of my Nation and my communities. . . . It is *why* I write. To make a whole. To take these splits forced upon us by racism, classism, homophobia, colourism, and baste them together" (81).

Gloria Anzaldúa defines identity, self-naming, and writing as ongoing processes. The importance of self-naming must be balanced with the awareness that accommodations must be made to avoid the creation of barriers and boundaries between different groups of people.

She emphasizes a creation of bridges, literal and symbolic, to facilitate community across cultural differences. Anzaldúa states, "I struggle with naming without fragmenting, without excluding. Containing and closing off the naming is the central issue of this piece of writing. . . . Identity flows between, over, aspects of a person. Identity is a river–a process" ("To(o) Queer the Writer" 252-253). The chorus of voices in this collection demonstrates the will to investigate self-identity within the immense array of differences that each individual embodies, and writing enables the individual to enter the "flow" of self-identification at many points in space and time. A respect for differences creates an enriched environment that proffers a sense of "reality" to all.

Many experiences create a distorted perspective on the self within time; recording events in writing preserves the experiences and opens them to introspective reality-seeking reflections. Audre Lorde names the "reality" created through the "act" of writing, however difficult and painful it is at the time; she describes the writing "process" as a strategy for healing:

> There is so much I have not said in the past few days, that can only be lived now–the act of writing seems impossible to me sometimes, the space of time for the words to form or be written is long enough for the situation to totally alter, leaving you liar or at search once again for the truth. What seems impossible is made real/tangible by the physical form of my brown arm moving across the page. (*Cancer Journals* 52)

Comments on the physical "act" of writing often bring into focus the physical presence of the writer, as well as the emotional and intellectual desires that powerfully generate the "act"; the body and the paper and the pen and the process meld into one. Beth Brant articulates the need to resist social silencing and to speak the realities that have been hidden from sight and knowledge; she names the need to write about other people's realities, as well, in order to provide witness: "Who do I protect with the secrets given me? / My pen is a knife. / I carve the letters BETTY OSBORNE on this yellow page. / Surely the paper must bleed from your name" (*Food & Spirits* 13). The body politic, the private body, and the body of the page spiral into one entity to demonstrate the difference that "telling" stories might make. Gloria Anzaldúa states, "In our common struggle, and in our writing we reclaim our tongues. We wield a pen as a tool, a weapon, a means of survival, a magic wand that will attract power, that will draw self-love into our bodies" ("Speaking In Tongues" 163).

As well as dealing with present circumstances, the "process" of self-writing, the immediate act of writing, provides an opportunity to revisit the past through an adult perspective. Writing in the immediate present provides the writer the ability to take partial control of the events during which they were potentially helpless and in fear–often fearing for their lives, as Marie Lovrod demonstrates in her doctoral dissertation investigation of sexual abuse narratives. The writing process not only creates a reality for the writer and helps to make the unspeakable take shape through words; during the material workings of the process the pain may be alleviated, or at least left aside for the moment through the pleasure, or even the distraction, of the writing process. "Acts" of self-writing may transform the pain into words of survival and power and agency, while integrating the experiences into present accountability.

Through ameliorative alteration, re-membering past events and putting them into written words of testimony often recuperates realities that may have been denied by the self or by others. In a writerly act that I define as "ameliorography," many authors powerfully enact a healing of the past through writing and taking the agency of self-expression. They bring together the past and the present in order to re-negotiate experiences and integrate the past into present selves-in-process. In a discussion of her work, along with the writings of other writers such as Janice Gould and Chrystos, Beth Brant notes that "Writing with our *whole* selves is an act that can re-vision our world. The use of erotic imaging in Native lesbian work becomes a tool by which we heal ourselves" (*Writing as Witness* 17).

Disclosure of violence and pain that disrupt individual personal lives opens up often-silenced social practices to interrogation. Native American poet Chrystos asks, "What is ethical to tell? This is especially complex when one is a part of oppressed groups, who stand to have any negative information used against them by the dominant-white-male-christian establishment" ("Askenet" 237). Cognizant of the ethical concerns that surround the "telling" of experience, lesbian autobiographical writings address many crucial issues, such as family dysfunction, homophobia in feminist movements, racism in society and in lesbian communities, the impact of childhood sexual abuse on adult sexuality, and homophobic treatment by health care and psychiatric professionals. Emily Driver and Audrey Droisen state, "Lesbianism among incest survivors is commonly treated professionally as a mental health problem rather than a positive adult choice" (*Child Sexual Abuse: Feminist Perspectives* 26). Mistreatment by medical and health care "professionals" is recorded by many lesbian writers, including Kate Millett, Chrystos, Anna Livia, Beth Brant, and Audre Lorde. According to Biddy Martin, writing openly about such personal subjects risks "possible subjection to surveillance, to the intervention of experts in our lives, to discipline" ("Feminism, Criticism, and Foucault" 8). Many lesbian writers declare that the risk must be taken in order to resist silencing of important parts of their lives and those of others, and to disrupt cycles of violence.

A complex set of risks is involved in the writing process that recalls past memories. Cathy Caruth comments on the commonly-experienced pain of recall and the nakedness of self-reflection on "the inability to fully witness the event as it occurs, or the ability to witness the event fully only at the cost of witnessing oneself" *(Trauma: Explorations in Memory* 7). Exemplifying the dynamic Caruth identifies, Gloria Anzaldúa notes,

> Because writing invokes images from my unconscious, and because some of the images are residues of trauma which I then have to reconstruct, I sometimes get sick when I do write. I can't stomach it, become nauseous, or burn with fever, worsen. But, in reconstructing the traumas behind the images, I make 'sense' of them, and once they have 'meaning' they are changed, transformed. It is then that writing heals me, brings me great joy. (*Borderlands* 70)

Gloria Anzaldúa connects writing with *making* "sense," and with the memories and knowledge held in the body. It is productive to interrelate the writers' attempts to find adequate metaphors to express the psychic and physical pain they have undergone, such as war/exile; wrestling/fencing; and wounds/scarring that make the body speak the unspeakable. The body becomes a text to be "read"; this becomes particularly important when there are no words adequate enough to describe the experience. Discussing the strife involved in the "coming together of two self-consistent but habitually incompatible frames of reference" and occupying a space of "perpetual transition" and "cultural collision," Anzaldúa states, "la mestiza undergoes a struggle of flesh, a struggle of borders, an inner war" (*Borderlands* 78).

The "struggle of flesh" involved in identity searches is a common experience that is related. The importance of the body in experiencing and articulating a sense of self is named explicitly. Representing the body as a medium of culture, as a social text (themes investigated by both Susan Bordo and Elizabeth Grosz), the writers in this collection not only read and write the body; they also identify sensory stimuli that trigger memories. The body and memory are constant motifs in lesbian self-writing. Nicole Brossard asserts, "Memory is a theatre of the body, representation's first theatre"; bringing together pain and joy, Brossard continues, "if we agree that a woman's memory is a memory inscribed in a marked body, if we agree that this memory is closely linked to a series of intimidations and repeated constraints in patriarchal time, then she who works the legend of the images and scenes churning in her will inevitably trace an explanatory map of the wounds and scars scattered over her body, as well as a map of the sudden rushes of joy that impassion thinking" ("Memory" 43). Brossard frankly illustrates the body as text to be read and she significantly foregrounds cultural inscriptions on the physical material body that are readily decipherable now and in the past. Identifying further dynamics in relation to memory, Mary Meigs notes, "My feeling now is that re-membering the heart is as important as re-membering the body, perhaps accompanies it" (letter to L. Hall, March 18, 1999).

Remembering past events and celebrating "rushes of joy" and also healing past pain are often acts that anticipate recognition by others. The self-authorship process provides reality and meaning for the self. The "act" of writing also invites witnesses, providing an imagined and then a potentially real community of understanding, and affirmation and confirmation through that understanding. Often a politically-motivated teaching impulse grounds motivational words that embrace others. Shoshana Felman and Dori Laub argue that

> The specific task of the literary testimony is, in other words, to open up in that belated witness, which the reader now historically becomes, the imaginative capability of perceiving history–what is happening to others–in one's own body, with the power of sight (of insight) usually afforded only by one's own immediate physical involvement. (*Testimony: Crisis of Witnessing in Literature* 15)

Embodied writings encourage an embodied reading process and response. Identification may occur on the physical level, as well as in the spiritual and emotional realms. Beth Brant deliberates the complex negotiations involved in "telling" her own stories and in "telling" the stories of others, particularly when it is often "not safe–being a writer" (*Food & Spirits* 14). She asks, "The ink of our own palette? / Medicine / Who will heal the writer who uses her ink and blood to tell? / Telling. / Who hears?" (15). She concludes this sequence with words of faith: "Love as honest as a poem. I have to tell. It is the only thing I know how to do" (17).

In "Art/i/fact: Rereading Culture and Subjectivity through Sexual Abuse Survivor Narratives," Marie Lovrod engages the crucial connection between the one "Telling" and the one "who hears." She suggests that the written record situates the reader as "a medium through which culture is forced to confront its own complicity" (23). Many of the writers in this collection elaborate on their sense of rereading their own lives through their writings; the writing and reading "process" makes sense and reality out of their lives, and it also provides witness for others. The reader recognizes personal complicity in the experiences of racism, homophobia, classism, ageism, and other painful acts that the writers divulge; thus, in response, the reader may become a "medium" for cultural change, as Lovrod suggests. Lovrod further addresses the self-reading and the spiralling reader/writer dynamic:

> The writer as reader of her or his own experience seeks to build a bridge between what Virginia Woolf describes as the violent shocks for which there have been no words and the reader of the survivor narrative so that the process of mediation between abuse and culture may proceed toward validation of the experience and transformation of the culture. (23)

This "bridging" act of writing provides exposure of culturally denied experiences, and often results in validation of the writer's experiences. As Beth Brant explains, "the need to tell and be believed" (*Food & Spirits* 16) is a driving impetus for many acts of self-writing, and acknowledgement by the reader is a significant transformational experience. According to Lovrod, a crucial component of social transformation is the requirement for the reader to become "responseable," to recognize the "writer's claims as reader of and authority" on the experiences of abuse that are related ("Art/i/fact" 30). Only through such responsible strategies is it possible to "appreciate the creative energy required to pronounce experiences that have been excluded from the cultural vocabulary" (30), Lovrod suggests. The reader, as witness to the writer's subjectivity, participates in cultural transformation through the "act" of seeing and hearing the "telling" of experiences. The term "life-writing" takes on new meaning when it is regarded in terms of writing the past into reality, and creating understanding and more favorable (and even possible) *living* conditions for the present and the future.

Writers' addresses to the future often indicate the affirmation and hope for their lives to come. They demonstrate their desires for social transformation and a change in the heteronormative, male-dominated status quo. Karla Jay deliberates the dangers and accusations that may accompany her frank revelations in *Tales of the Lavender Menace*. Instead of suffering in silence, Jay encourages others to speak out. She suggests that perhaps her book "will give them permission to speak of their pain without fear of condemnation. . . . I hope, in the original spirit of consciousness-raising, that my account will encourage others to give voice to their own" (265). In a similar vein, Audre Lorde writes, "May these words serve as encouragement for other women to speak and to act out of our experiences with cancer and with other threats of death, for silence has never brought us anything of worth. Most of all, may these words underline the possibilities of self-healing and the richness of living for all women" (*Cancer Journals* 10).

Writing often recuperates various desires, for the self, and for others. The celebrative and healing spiral is embodied in the web of writerly acknowledgements between Nicole Brossard, Betsy Warland, Mary Meigs, Kate Millett, Jane Rule, and many others who participated in this project. As well, the writers articulate the need for witnesses and they voice the affirmation they receive from readers' testimony-laden letters. Mary Meigs relates a circling dynamic that she experienced; a woman contacted Meigs after she saw her performance in the NFB film *The Company of Strangers* and had read one of Meigs' books, *The Time Being*. In *Moments of Being* Virginia Woolf states that "the shock-receiving capacity is what makes me a writer. I hazard the explanation that a shock is at once in my case followed by the desire to explain it" (72). Woolf suggests that the writing process facilitates an understanding of traumatic events from the past by making events "real": "It is only by putting it into words that I make it whole; this wholeness means that it has lost its power to hurt me; it gives me, perhaps because by doing so I take away the pain, a great delight to put the several parts together" (72). Mary Meigs comments on Woolf's words in relation to her own writing and self-understanding:

> My latest book is *The Time Being* and like the others is an attempt to make an experience whole by "putting it into words." (The quotation from *Moments of Being* came very close to my own reasons for writing.) It's the story of a love affair between two old (68 and 74) women, which begins in letters and continues when one of them goes to visit the other in Australia. Writing about such an experience is also a journey toward a more dispassionate understanding; in fact, that's the main challenge. (letter to L. Hall, February 4, 1999)

Lesbian writers often anticipate readers and express their desires to create social transformation through a politics of intervention. Profound in her honesty, Audre Lorde dismisses the risks involved in writing her self and asserts, "I had to remind myself that I had lived through it all, already. I had known the pain, and survived it. It only remained for me to give it voice, to share it for use, that the pain not be wasted . . . [she lives] knowing that within this continuum, my life and my love and my work has particular power and meaning relative to others" (*Cancer Journals* 16-17).

In a spiralling writer/reader dynamic, a community of knowing, understanding, and identification is created through words. A politics of intervention imbues the long writing careers of many of these authors. Kate Millett's *Sexual Politics,* published in 1969, powerfully interrogated the oppressive forces that came to bear on women's bodies and sexualities. Karla Jay's contemporary *Tales of the Lavender Menace* offers a historical review of women's political activism and the lesbian experiences within the various movements. Writers such as Beth Brant and Jewelle Gomez record the challenges of racism as it intersects with differences of sexuality, class, age, and geography. Ruthann Robson's *Sappho Goes to Law School* and several of her other writings address legal issues as they impact lesbian lives. Betsy Warland, Anna Livia, Lesléa Newman, Jess Wells, and Beth Brant elaborate on the politics and other institutional factors that impact experiences of lesbian motherhood. The frequent vein of humor that braces many of their writings attests to the potential of humour for social intervention, and as well, embodies the spirit necessary to thrive in a world full of possibilities, despite the barriers that must be overcome.

The "telling" of experience can be an empowering experience for writer and reader. Reclaiming control over their bodies and voices, lesbian writers produce and re-produce culture in order to participate in creating the present and future possibilities for all. Lesbian writers who address the "self" literally put their bodies on the line, and cross traditional borders separating the private and the public, the psyche and the social, and practical and theoretical considerations. They make their writing itself a part of their self-in-process. Nicole Brossard addresses the self, the body, and the body as sign, when she recalls a reading where the response and the community in the room was exhilarating; she writes,

> I felt the force of the energy circulating in the room. I understood that this current of energy was composed of the values and experiences criss-crossing in all directions of our lives. This energy, I could hear it vibrating in each and every one of us. It came from our tears, our orgasms, our laughter, and our wounds. This energy, I could hear it healing our lives. The magic of words was operating. It was building bridges between us. And on these bridges, we were going forward to meet our lives. (*Contemporary Authors* 52)

REFERENCES

Anzaldúa, Gloria. *Borderlands/La Frontera*. San Francisco: Spinsters/Aunt Lute Press, 1989.

_____ . "Speaking In Tongues: A Letter to 3rd World Women Writers." *This Bridge Called My Back: Writings by Radical Women of Color.* Ed. Cherríe Moraga and Gloria Anzaldúa. New York: Kitchen Table Press, 1983. 165-173.

_____ . "To(o) Queer the Writer—Loca, escritora y chicana." *Inversions: Writings by Dykes, Queers & Lesbians.* Ed. Betsy Warland. Vancouver: Press Gang, 1991. 249-261.

Brant, Beth. *Food & Spirits*. Vancouver: Press Gang, 1991.

_____ . *Writing as Witness: Essay and Talk.* Toronto: Women's Press, 1994.

Brossard, Nicole. *Aerial Letter*. Trans. Marlene Wildeman. Toronto: Women's Press, 1988.

_____. "Interview with Clea Notar." *Rubicon* 10 (Fall 1988): 173-195.

_____. "Memory: Hologram of Desire." *Trivia* 13 (1988): 42-47.

_____. "Nicole Brossard." *Contemporary Authors Autobiography Series.* Volume 16. Detroit: Gale Research, 1992. 39-57.

_____. *She Would Be the First Sentence of My Next Novel.* Trans. Susanne de Lotbinière-Harwood. Montreal: Mercury Press, 1999.

Cappello, Mary. *Night Bloom: A Memoir.* Boston: Beacon, 1998.

Caruth, Cathy, ed. *Trauma: Explorations in Memory.* Baltimore: Johns Hopkins UP, 1995.

Chrystos. "Askenet–Meaning 'Raw' in My Language." *Inversions.* 237-248.

de Lauretis, Teresa. *Technologies of Gender: Essays on Theory, Film, and Fiction.* Bloomington: Indiana UP, 1987.

Driver, Emily, and Audrey Droisen. *Child Sexual Abuse: Feminist Perspectives.* Basingstoke: Macmillan, 1989.

Felman, Shoshana, and Dori Laub. *Testimony: Crisis of Witnessing in Literature, Psychoanalysis and History.* New York: Routledge, 1992.

Grosz, Elizabeth. *Volatile Bodies: Toward a Corporeal Feminism.* Bloomington: Indiana UP, 1994.

Jay, Karla. *Tales of the Lavender Menace: A Memoir of Liberation.* New York: Basic, 1999.

Livia, Anna. *Pronoun Envy.* New York: Oxford UP, 2000.

Lorde, Audre. *The Cancer Journals.* San Francisco: Spinsters Ink, 1980.

Lovrod, Marie. "Literary Survivors: Issues in the Representation of Child Sexual Abuse." Diss. U of Calgary, 1996.

_____. "Art/i/fact: Rereading Culture and Subjectivity through Sexual Abuse Survivor Narratives." *True Relations: Autobiography and the Postmodern.* Ed. G. Thomas Couser and Joseph Fichtelberg. Westport, Conn.: Greenwood, 1998. 23-32.

Marlatt, Daphne. "Self-Representation and Fictionalysis." *Tessera* 8 (1990): 13-17.

Martin, Biddy. "Feminism, Criticism and Foucault." *Feminism and Foucault: Reflections on Resistance.* Eds. Irene Diamond and Lee Quinby. Boston: North Eastern University Press, 1988. 3-19.

Millett, Kate. *Flying.* New York: Ballantine, 1975.

Perreault, Jeanne. *Writing Selves: Contemporary Feminist Autography.* Minneapolis: University of Minnesota P, 1995.

Warland, Betsy. *What Holds Us Here.* Ottawa: Buschek, 1998.

Woolf, Virginia. *Moments of Being.* Ed. Jeanne Schulkind. 2d. ed. N.Y.: Harcourt Brace, 1985.

Writing Life

Beth Brant

SUMMARY. In her 1994 essay "Writing Life," Beth Brant discusses the role of writing in her life, the circumstances that surrounded her writing and editing endeavours, and her relationships with loved ones. Issues of racism, homophobia, and class oppression are explored through writing.

KEYWORDS. Lesbians, self-writing, body, racism, homophobia

I'm wondering if it might be a good time to make bread. The writing is not going well. Truthfully, it's not going. Perhaps the soothing action of mixing and kneading would get me back to a good place. The writing. the writing. It takes on large proportions in my mind. It is not easy to write. Nor is it fun, and pleasant is not a word I would use in conjunction with writing. Yet, it is hard to relax when I'm away

Beth Brant is a Bay of Quinte Mohawk from Tyendinaga Mohawk Territory in Ontario. Brant currently lives in Michigan. She is the editor of *A Gathering of Spirit,* the ground-breaking collection of writing and art by Native women (Firebrand Books, and Women's Press, 1988). She is the author of *Mohawk Trail,* prose and poetry (Firebrand Books, and Women's Press, 1985) and *Food & Spirits,* short fiction (Firebrand Books, and Press Gang, 1991). Her work has appeared in numerous Native, feminist and lesbian anthologies and she has done readings and lectures and taught throughout North America. Her latest book is *Writing As Witness: Essay and Talk* (Women's Press, 1994). "Writing Life" is the last essay in *Writing As Witness.*

Address correspondence to: Beth Brant, 18890 Reed, Melvindale, MI 48122 USA.

[Haworth co-indexing entry note]: "Writing Life." Brant, Beth. Co-published simultaneously in *Journal of Lesbian Studies* (Harrington Park Press, an imprint of The Haworth Press, Inc.) Vol. 4, No. 4, 2000, pp. 21-34; and: *Lesbian Self-Writing: The Embodiment of Experience* (ed: Lynda Hall) Harrington Park Press, an imprint of The Haworth Press, Inc., 2000, pp. 21-34.

from the computer and my desk. I keep thinking about the stories. I dream at night about the people in the stories. I see their faces in odd places–in the grocery store, on the street, sitting on a subway, lurking behind a tree or bush. They are like ghosts. But ghosts have had a life. These people are looking to me to help give them life.

In the kitchen I assemble the yeast, the flour, sugar, oil and take down the large stainless steel bowl. Turning on the tap, I empty two packets of yeast into the bowl. Running my wrist under the water to test the temperature, I judge it to be right. I measure two cups of water into the bowl. The yeast bubbles up, then sinks to the bottom.

This is a metaphor.

I stir the yeast and water with a wooden spoon and think about my dad. Daddy. I think of him often, missing him, wondering what he is doing in the Spirit World.

I add sugar, dry milk, and a little oil to the yeast-water. I stir, adding flour by the handful until the dough is a good consistency. I dump the mixture onto the cutting board and add still more flour to the spongy mass. I begin to knead–pushing it away with the heels of my hands, pulling it towards me–I make a rhythm.

When my dad was young, he discovered music–a certain kind of music. He was walking in a neighbourhood in Oshawa, Ontario, and heard music coming out of a window. He'd never heard music like that. He wanted to walk up to the house, ring the doorbell and ask what that music was. But he was a little Native boy, and little Native boys didn't ring doorbells and ask questions on a street that was white. He never said what he was doing on that particular street and I never asked–the story was enough.

The story is always good enough for me, but editors insist on explanations, details. Does it matter how he got from here to there? Does it matter? Isn't story why we are here, no matter the mode of transportation? Daddy said that when he grew up and was earning some money, he found out the name of the music he had heard on that Oshawa street–Beethoven's Ninth Symphony. He bought the record-ing, then a year later bought a record player, played it over and over, and sang "Ode to Joy" ever after. I like that story. It testifies to a number of things that Daddy taught me–beauty is possible, and beauty is found in unlikely places. All his stories were about that, all of my stories are about that.

I knead the bread and hum "Ode to Joy." I never planned on being a writer. It was not even a fantasy of mine. Born in an urban Mohawk family, story was a given, not something to search for or discover. But the gift of *writing* came a long time after my birth. Forty years after. That year I was on a search for the spirit of Molly Brant, Clan Mother, elder sister of Chief Joseph Brant and the architect of diplomatic relations between the Mohawk Nation and the British. My lover, Denise, and I were, at that time, caterers and bakers. We worked in our home (illegally) making desserts, quiche, breads, and various other items for small, local restaurants. We also were called upon to cater political events–conferences, seminars, benefits, readings, visual artists' openings. We did not make a lot of money, but enough to pay the bills and take care of our family, consisting of us and my three daughters. We had planned a camping trip in the East, stopping at Tyendinaga, my Reserve, then moving on to New York state. I wanted to visit all the homes in which Molly Brant had resided, just to see where she had walked, where she had slept, where she had dreamed. Her story has always been neglected in favour of her brother's, Joseph; just one more example of sexist racism at work. I didn't know what I was going to do with this knowledge or the feelings I would uncover, but I just wanted to *see* her with my own heart. Grandma Brant always told us that Molly was the true warrior and truth-carrier of the Brant history. We proceeded on our trip, stopping at Brantford, on to Six Nations to Tyendinaga (where Molly Brant never lived, but where my family did and does), on to New York state and the towns where Sir William Johnson and his "country wife" had made homes.

I wash out the bowl, oil it, and place the mound of kneaded dough inside, covering everything with a tea-towel. That trip changed my life, changed what image I had of myself; intensified my love of all things Native, all those things that make culture alive and real. It was while we were coming back to Michigan that we decided to take another road through what used to be Seneca land. The dirt road looped through strands of White Pine and deciduous growth. We were coming around a curve in the road, Denise driving, when a great shadow blocked out the sunlight and the tip of a wing touched the front windshield. A Bald Eagle made his presence known to us. Denise stopped the car, I opened the door and stood, transfixed, as Eagle made a circle around us then flew to a nearby White Pine and settled himself on a branch. The branch dipped low from his weight, his dark wings folded around him, his white head touched by a flash of sunlight through the needles of the tree. I remember how his great talons gripped the branch as I moved closer and stood in front of him, my heart drumming inside my human body. We were locked together in vision. I could feel his heartbeat take over mine. I felt my hands curving and holding onto the branch. I felt the sunlight flashing on my head. I heard the thoughts; the deep, scratching thoughts of blood, bone and prey, the thoughts of wind carrying me along, the thoughts of heartbeat. He blinked his eyes, unfolded his wings, and flew away. I watched him as I slowly came back to myself, to the smell around me, the breeze picking up and scattering dust in my face, my legs growing so weak I could hardly walk back to the car. When I got home, I began to write.

I was born in 1941, in the house of my Grandma and Grandpa Brant–the house where my Aunt Colleen still lives. It was a hot May morning, as my Irish-Scots mother pushed and willed me out of her womb. The story goes that Daddy had brought an ice-cream-on-a-stick for my mom, but in the excitement, put it in his pocket. It wasn't until Grandma was doing the wash that she discovered the mess and made Daddy wash his own pants. I grew up in a family that had strong women and sweet men. Mama's family was not thrilled to have her marry an Indian, in fact her father refused to give her away at the wedding and railed and stormed about having a "nigger" for a son-in-law. In time he came around, but those kinds of wounds were not easy to close or heal.

I have a photograph of my mom and dad around the time they were newly married. They were ages eighteen and twenty. The old black and white photograph shows my mom wearing shorts and a halter top, Daddy dressed in a short-sleeved shirt and pants. They are leaning against a honeysuckle vine, Daddy's arms around Mama's bare waist. She is leaning against his chest, head thrown back with laughter. She is holding his hands that encircle her waist. They look so young, so sensual, so in love, so happy to be touching and smelling the honey-suckle that twists around Daddy's dark hair and comes to rest on Mama's blonde head. I came from this–this union of white and Native.

Mama and Daddy came to live with the Brant family. In the old way, the traditional way, Daddy would have gone to live with the Smiths. But since Mama was a white woman and feelings were bad on their side, it was the natural course of things that the Brants would assimilate her and all offspring of the union. Thus, I was born in the Little Room of Grandma and Grandpa's house in Detroit, the room that was alternately used as a birthing room, a sick room, a room to put up various members of the family when they came to visit or to live.

Memories are stories–pictures of the mind, gathered up and words put to them, making them live and breathe. My memories are good ones. I was loved.

There were a lot of us, living in that small house. Grandma, Grandpa, Auntie, Mom and Dad, and their three children. At other times there were more–aunts, uncles and their children, relatives from Tyendinaga with their families. I wonder to this day how we all fit, how we managed to all sit around the kitchen table. (The young kids usually ate in the Little Room off a card table. It was a rite of passage when we became old enough to sit with the grown-ups. Like most of what Grandma did, she had her own way of deciding who was old enough. I think I sat with the adults when I turned twelve, but others got there before their twelfth year, and some had to wait much longer.) When my cousins and I get together, we inevitably get around to talking about that card table and the question of space. How did we all fit? Was there some magic involved?

There were books. Both Grandma and Grandpa knew how to read and write. They considered it a blessing. They read a lot and always bought the newspaper. Grandma was a Methodist and read a verse from the Bible every night before she went to bed. And she insisted on saying grace before meals. "Our heavenly father, we ask you to bless this food for the use of our souls and bodies. In Jesus' name we ask it. Amen." Grandpa was not a christian, preferring the old way, the Mohawk way. Yet, for all of Grandma's high-mindedness about christianity, she believed most fervently in the power and beauty of Earth. Her garden was a testament to that belief.

The first inklings of connection and intimacy with Land came from watching and helping Grandma and Grandpa work the garden. Getting the soil ready, using the planting stick, seeds drifting from their hands, I felt the devotion and care they lavished on that small piece of land. When we would take trips to Tydendinaga (our Territory and the place they were born and raised) I felt that connection even more deeply. This is where they came from. This is where Daddy came from. This is where I came from. This is where our people's bones are buried and revered. This is *home*.

Grandpa taught me Mohawk and the idea of what men are supposed to be–loving, hard workers, giving, secure, respectful of women, playful with children. Grandma taught me manners, how to make corn soup and fry bread, and the idea of what women are supposed to be–strong, fierce protectors of family and land, independent of men while respecting them. (If they warranted respect. She held no affection for men who drank, neglected family, or hurt children and women.) Grandma never needed a man to tell her how to fix a toilet, clean a well, or butcher a deer. And her daughters, my aunts, followed her counsel. Even my mother became like that. She must have gathered the knowledge by osmosis. Those two grandparents formed many of my values and the beliefs I hold to.

I get up to check the bread. It has a smooth, glossy look to it. I poke my finger in gently and the bread rises up to cover the hole. I punch it down, cut it in two pieces, make two loaves and place them in the bread pans.

When I began to write, I wrote about my family. At first there were funny stories about my grandparents' Indian ways. Nice stories, full of loving description of their ways with each other and with the world outside them. Then something happened. The writing got more serious; my family was not just fun–they were also survivors of colonial oppression. I began to figure out, through the writing, that what I remembered was not necessarily the complete truth. I was still viewing the family through the eyes of the child I had been.

What happens when I sit in front of the computer (or, in those days, the typewriter)? This desire to peel back the husk of memory, the hungry need to find the food that is waiting inside. There are times when I feel as if *I* am the seed, being watered and sunned by the keys I press to make words. The words are the shoot, wandering across the screen, stopping then starting, coming from my mouth, my fingers. I speak aloud as I write–the words being borne from mouth to hand. Somewhere in that activity is the nucleus of writing, of truth. I no longer feel that the words come directly from me. There are spirits at work who move my lips, my fingers. Who call me, who take over my clumsy attempts to put one word after the other to make some kind of sense. An automatic writing of sorts. I used to fight the spirits. Now I accept them.

I check the loaves. They have risen nicely. I place them in the oven at 375 degrees, close the door and think about the work that is piled on my desk. There are deadlines for articles, correspondence to write, a book to finish, another book making itself known at the edges of my mind. I procrastinate. I avoid the inevitable confrontation with the spirits of writing. I have been known to clean the whole house to the extent of cleaning cupboards, just to keep from doing what the screen asks me to reveal. Why? At this point in my life, I have written about most things that others would shy away from–my life with an abusive, alcoholic husband, my life with Denise, my lesbianism, sexual lovers– yet, there is always the modesty, and the fear of being judged and therefore, all Mohawks being judged. The writing spirit has no fear, has no human failings that waste time procrastinating. There are times when I think the spirit is the collected consciousness of those Native writers who have passed on–Pauline Johnson, D'Arcy McNickle; they can't stop writing, even in the Spirit World, and have to make visitations to those of us on Earth who call ourselves writers. And while I have accepted their presence in my life, I still want to ask–why me? They do not answer.

There was a time when I was ashamed to be Indian. This happened around the time I was in the fifth or sixth grade. I was a pale, blonde child, I wore glasses, and had lots of baby fat. Until then, I was ashamed of my lightness, my paleness. The family was dark–dark skin, dark hair, dark eyes–and then there was me. I used to wonder if I was the right child, or if I was somehow switched at birth. Since I was born at home and there were no other babies around, this fantasy didn't last long. I was very jealous of my cousins who "looked" Mohawk. They had the dark hair I envied, the brown or dark eyes I wanted to peer out of my own face. I resented my mother–somehow this was her fault. But as I grew older and caught the drift of racism, I hid my Mohawk self from the schoolmates who might have become my tormenters, had they known. It was enough that I was fat and wore glasses; taunting and teasing waited for me if I made myself noticed. At home, life went on pretty much as usual. The family was not aware of my "other life" as a white girl. My girlfriends in the neighborhood didn't give a whole lot of thought to the family. Anyway, they had grown up on the street that had the only Indian family. This was nothing new or different to them. But the other kids in school were to be feared, cajoled, envied.

My writing soon took an autobiographical bent. I got published fairly soon, a fact that causes me amazement even today. My work in those days was raw, not as free from cliché or roughness, but editors saw something. There was a substantial network of feminist journals and magazines in the early 80s. They took chances on women like me–women who had no prior publishing experience, women who were not "educated," women of colour. Taking chances was the hallmark of these publications, and I am very thankful for their existence.

It seemed to me that Eagle had many plans for me. In 1982, I was asked to edit a special issue of *Sinister Wisdom,* a feminist journal at that time published and edited by Adrienne Rich and Michelle Cliff. I took on the job, not because I knew anything about editing, but because the issue was to be about Native women. This caused me a lot of excitement *and* fear. In the first place, until that time, there had not been an anthology of exclusively Native women's work. All other Native anthologies had been edited by whites. *A Gathering of Spirit* was a ground-breaker in those two areas, but also in another equally important area. Of the sixty women who had contributed to the book, ten of us declared our lesbianism. This was a new day in the history of Aboriginal writing. This time around, we were actively saying who we were–all parts of us–no coyness, or hiding, or pretending to be something we weren't. It was a great political and personally courageous act on the part of those nine women who stood with me. I will always be thankful to them and blessed in knowing them.

Another wonderful thing about *A Gathering of Spirit* is the humanness of the book. This is not just another anthology of well-known and well-published authors. There are first-time writers, voices from Native women in prison, letters, oral histories, artwork. This was a special book in 1983. It continues to be a special book today. Native women write to tell me how the book changed their lives. Many of the women who were published for the first time, now have their own books. And many Two-Spirits thank me for shaking the stereotype of what makes good writing, what makes good Native writing–it is not all male, or heterosexual, or necessarily from the pen of someone who had formal western education. I am very proud of that book. Not because I edited it, but because it changed the face of Native literature forever. It became its own entity. It became what it had to be–a brilliant and loving weapon of change.

I published my first book of poems and stories, *Mohawk Trail,* in 1985. Although I like this book and continue to read some of the work in public performance, I am always chagrined when people mention a piece from it. I want to say, "That old stuff," not because I don't like the work, but because each *new* work seems better to me, more full and mature. Perhaps this is the way with writers. My book of short stories, *Food & Spirits,* was published in 1991. There was a long gap between books because I am not a prolific writer. I do not write every day, yet I write in my head every day. I listen to people's conversations, not because I am a voyeur, but because I am fascinated with people's voices–the rhythm, the phrases they use, the accents, the music. I keep these some place inside me; even in sleep, words from a conversation flash by; people's faces pop up, some I've never seen before. Linda Hogan once said that she used to think she was crazy, but then she realized that the craziness was due to being a half-breed in a white world. I believe that too. I also believe that being a Native writer induces its own madness. We are trying to make sense out of the senseless. We are trying to tell a truth in a culture that dishonours truth-tellers and the story behind the telling.

Grandpa died when I was quite young. I remember the wake, his body laid out in the wooden box, the family and strangers all over the place. I hated it. It scared me. I wasn't quite sure that he was really dead, or if he would rise up (like one of the stories in Grandma's bible). If Grandpa was really dead, who would talk with me in Mohawk? (By one of those generational twists, a result of colonialism, my father and his siblings didn't speak the language, but understood it. I suspect that Grandma had a lot to do with this. Although she remained adamantly and vehemently Mohawk, she also felt that it was okay to assimilate "a little," for safety's sake.) If Grandpa was really dead, how would we all survive? We depended on him for so much, not just economically, but emotionally and spiritually. Who would counteract Grandma's forays into Christian platitudes? Who would hug me tight and call me his "masterpiece"? Who would make the raspberry jam every year, the bright red jars decorating the fruit cellar?

Grandma died when I was eighteen, newly married and a mother. My husband had been in the Navy and we were living in a forsaken town in Georgia. There was no money for me to come home, so the family decided they wouldn't tell me about the death until after the wake. I was furious. I felt that I was given no choice. It's true there was no money, but I would have liked to have said goodbye to Grandma at her moment of death, not after she was in the ground. It was years before I found myself at the cemetery where they both were buried. It had taken me that long to be able to see that place, that land of death. And many years after that, I took my two oldest grandsons, Nathanael and Benjamin, to visit. They rolled on the markers, picked up leaves and threw them at each other, shouted and laughed. I wondered how often a cemetery gets to hear the laughter of children. I tell my grandsons about their great-great-grandparents. My memory will shift to theirs, and they will keep the stories alive and moving.

My marriage was not a good one. I was seventeen and pregnant. My dad didn't want me to marry. My mom did. She often would have these attacks of caring what people thought of her. I suppose her great rebellion in marrying my dad took its toll on her in little ways. She would compensate by drilling us in proper behaviour and morals. I don't know what I wanted. I guess I wanted to be grown-up and living a grown-up life. I thought that marriage guaranteed that. Also, my mom and dad genuinely loved and liked each other. I had no idea that my husband wasn't a sweet Mohawk man. We were to live out the fourteen years together in anger, violence, alcohol, hatred. But I had three daughters, Kimberly, Jennifer, Jill; and they were in turn the only sweetness and beauty that was visible to me during those fourteen years.

Leave him I did; or rather, told him to leave us. I went on welfare, looked for work, tried to hold it together. My parents were wonderful–buying food, buying the kids' clothes, taking care of things when I felt I couldn't. They had always been there during the course of my marriage, but I couldn't bring myself to tell them just how many times he came home drunk, the marital rape, the screaming and shouting. I was ashamed to tell them, as if *I* had brought this to be. Daddy, slow to anger, would have erupted and probably done harm to my husband and brought harm to himself. My mother would have wanted to find a way to take care of it that would reduce me to a child again. I kept all of it secret, only daring, years later, to expose the secrets through writing.

I do not believe that all writing is autobiographical, or that a writer has to use words as a confessional. In fact, I think that type of writing is unique to white North America. I do know that as a Mohawk woman, I was born to and grew up in a culture that persists and resists, but also carries its load of colonialist untruths. As an Aboriginal woman, I have internalized these untruths. Writing helps me to let go. The spirits of writing bring comfort, assurance, righteous anger, deliverance. I am alive, quivering, in front of the computer. I dredge but also bury. I face the monsters of racism, homophobia, woman-hating, with the spirits beside me. I am protected at the same time as I open myself to rage. I find salvation while uncovering horror. Writing is the place to feel all senses commingle and cohabit, bringing forth something new, giving birth to words, to beings that will inhabit story, that *are* story. This is what the spirits bring–verdant sensuality, lush panoply, a garden.

I check the bread. It is rising, developing a golden crust. It is almost done, almost there.

I met Denise Dorsz in 1976. I immediately loved her. For me, it was simple–I wanted to make a life with this woman. I wanted to share my life with her. Denise has brought many gifts into my life; we have also had to struggle and fight for the ability of each of us to be separate and unique while building a partnership of love and continuity. Denise is white–Polish-American–and is also twelve years younger than me. The romanticising of the lesbian and gay community is hard to dispel. We often believe the myth that is not exclusive to heterosexuality–fall in love, live happily ever after. As of this writing, in 1994, we have been together for eighteen years. There was a period of time when we were separated, and I wrote exhaustively and excessively during that time about our relationship, about our separation. None of this was for publication, but then, none of what I write is consciously or unconsciously for anyone else but me and the spirits. My point is that I was able to use writing to heal a wound that was very deep and festering. I was angry–writing brought me calm. I was obsessing about the past–writing gave me insight into the future. I was in pain–writing cooled the pain, brought me out of that condition. Writing was/is Medicine. It is the only thing I know that brings complete wholeness while it is making a visitation. Making love comes close–orgasm, like writing, is a spiritual communication.

I never went to university. My circumstances were such that it was unthinkable to even imagine going. Yet, my father had worked days in the auto factory and gone to college at night. Formal education was not unheard of or dismissed in the family. My grandparents thought highly of it, Daddy and Mama worked tirelessly to achieve it for my father. My siblings and I were encouraged, prodded to achieve a degree of some kind, and my sister and brother worked extremely hard to get those degrees. Instead, I married and gave up all desires for expansion of myself. It was 1959; this is what women did, especially self-hating ones like me. Why did I hate myself? There is no simple political polemic that can explain or describe my actions. I was loved by my family. I had solid and sturdy role models. I had culture. I had language. I had a spiritual base. Then again, I inherited secrets. They wore me down. I learned to be silent, rather than reveal the family I wanted to idealize.

The secrets of Indigenous life are not secret. Alcoholism, family violence, the internalized violence of self-doubt, self-loathing. My father, who was a brilliant man, used to say in serio-comic fashion, "What do I know, I'm just a dumb Indian." He knew he wasn't, yet *did not know* if he was just that. I have also made that statement, but more than that, I have thought it and felt it. Writing has changed my perception of myself. Eagle has changed my way of being in this life.

Writing. This mysterious and magical act that brings possibility of transformation. I do not believe that what I have to say is more important than others' words. At the same time, there is a reason why I am able to bead words together to make language. It makes me able to be of use: to my people, to the many families I am connected to–First Nations, feminist, gay and lesbian, working-class, human. I love words. When I was in the sixth grade, I won a spelling-bee and my prize was a dictionary. I loved that book–so many words to choose from, so many words to play with. To this day, I write with a dictionary beside me, sometimes forgetting what I'm writing as I turn the pages of that book, reading the meanings, the way words came into being. Yet, there are times when English words are not full enough or circular enough to encompass a thought or feeling I am trying to convey. It is then that I mourn for the loss of my Mohawk language. With no one to speak it with after Grandpa died, I have forgotten the words, but not the wholeness and richness of the meaning behind the words. I believe my language is hovering somewhere inside the place where the writing spirits dwell. They will bring it back to me. And there are times when Mohawk words jump into the computer, a surprise, a lovely gift when I least expected them to come.

I loved to read. I began reading at age four, taught by Grandpa and my dad. I remember the book, *Johnny Had a Nickel,* a book about a kid who had a nickel to spend and the long list of things he could buy with it (this was 1945, don't forget). Johnny ended up going for a ride on a carousel, but I ended up with an obsession for words, and a great respect for books. I had a library card when I was five. The library was fascinating to me–still is. I thought people who wrote books were creatures different from us. I didn't know until I was well into adulthood that Native people wrote books, and that Pauline Johnson, a Mohawk writer, had been published in the last century. My family didn't know either, or we would have had those books in our home. I read everything and anything I could get my hands on. It's cliché, but books were my friends. Along with movies, they shaped my view of the society I lived in. I always knew that my family was not a part of that society, didn't *want* to be a part of that society. Ah, but how *I* wanted to be (at least during my childhood and teen-age years). I wanted to be an actress like Ava Gardner, Rita Hayworth; I wanted to dance like Marge Champion, sing like Ella Fitzgerald or June Christy (I seemed to have a lot of confusion about where my loyalties lay–with the white girls or the women of colour! Maybe this is what being a half-breed means). I wanted to be acceptable. It wasn't until I was grown that I picked up a book by James Baldwin, and found the kind of words and world that had meaning for me, personally. Though he wrote from the culture of African-Americans, he wrote about the effects of racism, the effects of colonialism, and I found the missing words that had left me bereft of meaning in my life. Later on, I was to "discover" Scott Momaday, James Welch, Simon Ortiz, Paula Gunn Allen–people of my own kind, people who wrote about *us*.

The timer is ringing. The bread-smells are permeating the house. I open the oven, the heat fogging my glasses. For a moment, I can't see, caught in another way of being. I lift my head, hearing the faint whispers of spirits gathering together. My glasses clear, I remove the bread from the oven, tapping it, hearing that hollow sound that signifies a good loaf of bread. I turn the loaves onto the counter and return to the computer. I turn it on–a low hum emits as I tap in the code to lay the screen bare and accepting.

In most of my work, especially the short stories, I attempt to show break-throughs in people's lives. Much of my own life has involved breaking through existing scenarios that have been programmed into my head. Despite the loving and culturally rich messages I received from the family, the cacophony of the dominant society made an even louder noise. Through writing, I "come back" to the family, come back to who I am, and *why* I am. The noise of dominance recedes and gives over to the music of my ancestors, my history. The people who inhabit my stories, inhabit my life. They have made a home inside me, inside the computer, on the page. The people who live in story are, like Native people everywhere, struggling and dreaming, caught between the beauty of what we know, and the ugliness of what has been done to our people, our land. It seems as though I give these people choices–like the choice I make every day–to resist the ugly and go with the beauty. I say, "it seems," because I never know what the people are going to do; they tell me. I feel as though they are speaking, "Write me, write me," and I have to struggle against what I have been told from white society, free myself, and give myself over to the singing and whispering that is my world, the world of Indigenous being.

When I was finishing up a book of essays, my father, whose physical body died in 1991, came to sit with me. My father, who never wrote a book, but wanted to, oh how he wanted to, was with me, chastising me over sentences that wouldn't live, "Now, Bella, you know that doesn't sound right," praising me when I got it right, "That's good, Daughter, that's good." His life, which was often so circumscribed, was one of hope and faith. He believed in the continuation of the People. He believed in the old way, the *Onkwehonwe* way. He believed that the best was always to come. He left Earth with that faith gleaming in his eyes, transported to the Spirit World where he probably sings "Ode to Joy" to his relatives. It is my turn, my inheritance to sing an ode to the continuity of Mohawk ethos.

The bread is made. Later on tonight, Denise and I will cut it, slather on the butter, the same butter I am told is bad for my arteries. I'll save some for my grandsons, four examples of how story continues in the blood.

The computer is humming. The cursor blinks and talks, calling me into the sacred territory of story and meaning. They are gathering forcefully now, the alchemy is about to begin. Alchemy–from the Greek word Khemia, meaning Black Land–the Black Land of these words appearing on an electronic machine, soon to be transmuted into words on paper, the flesh of trees. What happens after, no longer has to do with me. I've done my job.

A State of Mind in the Garden

Nicole Brossard

SUMMARY. Nicole Brossard reflects on the writing process in relation to self, narrative voice, language, translation, lesbian desire and sexuality, genre-blurring, memory, and the cultural milieu. She explores her resistant negotiations of traditional autobiographical modes of writing. *[Article copies available for a fee from The Haworth Document Delivery Service: 1-800-342-9678. E-mail address: <getinfo@haworthpressinc.com> Website: <http://www.HaworthPress.com>]*

KEYWORDS. Lesbians, self-writing, body, language, memory

Je ne consens à livrer mes rêves que dans l'absolu du plaisir, dans le degré zéro qui menace toutes les interprétations et qui pourtant les initie comme autant de rêves.

Nicole Brossard is a poet, novelist, and essayist. She has published more than thirty books since 1965. Works that have been translated into English include *She Would Be the First Sentence of My Next Novel* (Mercury, 1998), *Mauve Desert* (Coach House, 1990), *Surfaces of Sense* (Coach House, 1989), *The Aerial Letter* (Women's Press, 1988), *Lovhers* (Guernica, 1987), *Sous la Tongue/Under Tongue* (Gynergy, 1987), *French Kiss* (Coach House, 1986), *Journal Intime* (Herbes rouges, 1984), *These Our Mothers* (Coach House, 1983), and *Daydream Mechanics* (Coach House, 1980). She co-founded the literary magazine *La Barre du Jour* (1965-1975). She is twice winner of the Canadian Governor General Award for poetry in French, for *Mecanique jongleuse* (1975), and *Double Impression* (1984). She was awarded, in 1989, *Le Grand Prix de poésie de la Fondation Les Forges*.

Both excerpts in French are from *Journal intime* suivi de *Oeuvre de chair et métonymies,* Montréal, Herbes rouges, 1998. A first edition of *Journal intime* was published in 1984.

Address correspondence to: Nicole Brossard, 34 Ave Robert, Outremont, Quebec, Canada H3S 2P2.

[Haworth co-indexing entry note]: "A State of Mind in the Garden." Brossard, Nicole. Co-published simultaneously in *Journal of Lesbian Studies* (Harrington Park Press, an imprint of The Haworth Press, Inc.) Vol. 4, No. 4, 2000, pp. 35-40; and: *Lesbian Self-Writing: The Embodiment of Experience* (ed: Lynda Hall) Harrington Park Press, an imprint of The Haworth Press, Inc., 2000, pp. 35-40. Single or multiple copies of this article are available for a fee from The Haworth Document Delivery Service [1-800-342-9678, 9:00 a.m. - 5:00 p.m. (EST). E-mail address: getinfo@haworthpressinc.com].

Nicole Brossard
Photo by Germaine Beaulieu. Used by permission.

C'est la moindre des choses que de ne pas avoir à faire tous les jours la preuve qu'on existe. C'est le moindre des choses quoique je connaisse des millions de femmes qui chaque jour doivent en faire la preuve. Certaines crient, d'autres grimacent, d'autres se tordent de rire, d'autres se frottent les mains comme pour en faire jaillir le feu, d'autres pensent qu'une existence remplie de mots c'est comme un trou noir dans le cosmos; d'autres disent qu'exister c'est parler dans la matière ou encore qu'exister c'est tracer un chemin avec sa bouche et son souffle dans l'infini recommencé de la matière.

1.

Cultures come and go. A great number of languages and species have died, others are disappearing at an incredible speed. War goes on non-stop around the world. A new civilization has started to change our notion of time, of space; is shaping differently our use of memory, of knowledge; is modifying the way humans, animals and vegetation reproduce; is altering our certitudes about nature and the future. Yet most of the women living on this earth are enduring a non-human condition because they do not qualify as hu*man*. Life goes on, you travel, you make love, your mother dies, old friends pass away. One day you are asked to write about the self, yourself, your lesbianself and what writing can do for you. Suddenly you realize that more than anything else you are into life as others are into business.

2.

The world is changing. From memory to plain information, from depth to surface, from the reign of symbols to the reign of signs. The world is changing. Water is becoming rare and rarer. Yet I am sitting in the garden writing an article still tracing letters with ink and pen, enjoying *le chant des cigales*, wondering if I will write about love, sex, memory or real life. But I know that I can only write about one thing: how strongly I feel *l'immensité* in my chest and how this feeling is related to the virtuality of language. A virtuality which I cannot help associating with the idea of *making sense*. Making sense of life, of *l'immensité* in us, encountering the electrifying pleasure that sex, love, art and nature offer us as well as making sense of death, no matter whatever its course in our life.

3.

Playing with words, enjoying them, craving them or searching desperately for the appropriate ones to translate "*un*believable" experiences are situations in which I have found myself throughout my writing life. As I have often said, I do not see myself as a witness of my life or that of others. I see myself as an explorer in language who is trying to discover new territories. I work with language hoping that it will enable me to produce and offer sequences of emotions and thoughts which, without the written word, would not exist.

4.

I do not write to *indulge myself,* to attenuate pain, anger or a sense of injustice. Of course, anything that is painful in my life will affect my writing. Even though it might orient my thoughts toward new themes, pain will not produce in me a desire to give in to anecdotes. Mostly it will affect the energy I am usually relying on or using in my exploration of meaning. Pain and pleasure are known to affect our breath when encountered in a vital way in life and they certainly transform the rhythm of my texts. Anything vividly experienced by the body shapes our writing and the meaning we give to life.

5.

Being a poet, a novelist, and an essayist allows me to acknowledge and process differently emotions and events traversing my life. Here, I think of the cycle: *Lovhers* (poetry), *Picture Theory* (novel) and *The Aerial Letter* (essays). Processing the raw material of desire and of sexual attraction into metaphors and the language of symbols is what poetry often does. In that sense it is very different from revisiting emotions still alive in the inner landscape of the self, hoping (as we do in prose) that they will engender a narrative voice rich with what imagination and reality are able to produce when they have altered each other to converge into fiction. Processing emotions and facts into ideas or theory also calls for another posture. Expanding the meaning of your story into the realm of social values and ideology requires that you understand where and why your story does not fit into the system and standard values. By doing so, you are forced to reevaluate the dominant forces that prevent your story from existing loudly and clearly in the public forum.

6.

Of course, it is not that simple: and in my case, genres are blurred because strong emotions in me always bring up the need to understand their source, their patterns and their mechanics. Understanding is therefore a keyword in my work and this is how, for example, in the seventies and earlier eighties, while I was writing on utopia and ecstatic lesbian relationships, I was at the same time trying to figure out the tricky patriarchal logic which has been and is still so damaging to women, hoping that, once understood, it could free women at least from guilt and the double-bind.

7.

In the book *She Would Be the First Sentence of My Next Novel* (Mercury Press, 1998), I talk about my resistance to anecdote, diary, autobiography, while acknowledging the role those forms of writing have played in women's lives, be they writers or readers. I say that my *reserve* when it comes to writing down my life constitutes my *reserve* of images, of hope and of energy. I also say that my resistance to writing down my lived experience is a way to *reserve* myself for the essential, the intuited matter that would take the form of what I would later call *theoretical fiction*.

8.

I am fascinated by the fact that no matter what our politics and our solidarities are, or our obvious belongings (gender, race, culture), one's real identity and motivations are activated by a much more complex and profound scenario than those we use for political purposes.

9.

One is first lesbian because of the pleasure shaping the intelligence and the recognition that the other woman, *she* makes sense. Lesbian desire must remain free, open and nomadic, for it is by exploring that desire that our power to interact in the symbolic field takes effect.

10.

In the middle of our ideological discussions, *isn't each of us eager to ask* two questions of the other lesbian: when and how was it the first time? As if we need to hear about the origin, the founding moment in which we can retrace the illumination, the moment of passage when we suddenly found ourself on the other side of the mirror, of the world, in a universe where surprised, stunned and relieved, we could observe *our self* drifting away from Adam's coast. Questions starting with where and how are questions that resemble those often asked of writers. When did you start writing? Why do you write? What is autobiographical in your books? As if being a lesbian is associated with something as mysterious, desirable and creative as writing is.

11.

On the *Lesbian,* women and dykes can project what they don't know yet about themselves as well as what they already know. The *Lesbian* is a proposition and her proposition is sexual. Because that proposition is sexual, it astonishes and questions the good sense and the usual rationale. Her proposition questions sexual grammar, blurs the points of reference in sexual fantasies, and invites *au voyage.* It is because the lesbian's proposition is sexual that *she* has a symbolic effect, that it is illuminating.

12.

There will always be a risk that a text written by a lesbian might not be a lesbian text. While the lesbian text is linguistically constructed around a sexual proposition opening the space for other propositions to exist, the text written by a lesbian mostly relies on what she projects of her self. Her text becomes a lesbian text only if it alters the reader's sense of imagination.

"Demain ne me demandez pas ce que fut, ce que sera ma vie.

Demain, il y a mon effroyable prétention à la lucidité."

Voices in the Outer Room

Mary Cappello

SUMMARY. An argument (in the form of a demonstration) for the development of a queer aesthetic, the essay asks whether it is our charge as lesbian writers to hold a mirror up to our experience, to "self-disclose" (so often such narratives change nothing but succeed in flattening our lives), or to find the form that will answer to queer habits of being, radical sensibilities and ideologies. The essay takes three different liminal spaces as its ground–a sickroom, a conversation on an airplane, and a Catholic confessional–to explore my own aesthetic process, the role played by randomness and interruption in that process, the complex presence of external and internalized (dis)embodied voices in my self-writing, and the desire through my work to create what I call "disruptive beauty." *[Article copies available for a fee from The Haworth Document Delivery Service: 1-800-342-9678. E-mail address: <getinfo@haworthpressinc.com> Website: <http://www.HaworthPress.com>]*

KEYWORDS. Lesbian, queer, memoir, voice, aesthetics, confessional discourse, family

---

Mary Cappello, Associate Professor of English at the University of Rhode Island, is the author of *Night Bloom: A Memoir* (Beacon Press, 1998, published in paperback by Beacon Press in 1999 under the title *Night Bloom: An Italian American Life*). This volume is a multi-genre work that combines oral history, folklore, the bilingual journals of her Italian immigrant grandfather (a shoemaker by trade), dream-work, letters and cultural theory. Her creative non-fiction, including "My Mother Writes the Letter that I Dream," "Nothing to Confess," "Shadows in the Garden," and "Useful Knowledge," appears in numerous anthologies that consider the intersections of ethnic, class, and sexual identities. Her poetry has appeared in *The American Poetry Review, The Painted Bride Quarterly, The Paterson Literary Review,* and *Radical Teacher.* She is currently at work on a collection of experimental portraits, *The Truth in Faces,* about the forms that friendship takes between gay men and lesbians.

With special thanks to Karen Carr, Caeli Carr-Potter, and Karla Jay. This piece is indebted to Irving Berlin's *Easter Parade* and Barbara Hammer's *Women I Love.*

Address correspondence to: Mary Cappello, 27 Willow Street, Providence, RI 02909 USA (e-mail: mcapp@uri.edu).

[Haworth co-indexing entry note]: "Voices in the Outer Room." Cappello, Mary. Co-published simultaneously in *Journal of Lesbian Studies* (Harrington Park Press, an imprint of The Haworth Press, Inc.) Vol. 4, No. 4, 2000, pp. 41-58; and: *Lesbian Self-Writing: The Embodiment of Experience* (ed: Lynda Hall) Harrington Park Press, an imprint of The Haworth Press, Inc., 2000, pp. 41-58. Single or multiple copies of this article are available for a fee from The Haworth Document Delivery Service [1-800-342-9678, 9:00 a.m. - 5:00 p.m. (EST). E-mail address: getinfo@haworthpressinc.com].

Mary Cappello
Photo by Lina Pallotta. Used by permission.

I begin where I am. And, eventually, given that seeming tautology, granted enough patience to sit with uncertainty, I arrive, through writing, at something other than a circle. Or at least that is what is hoped. In writing, the world, "experience," becomes available in new ways, asking to be re-made, especially if that experience is, at first and persisting glance, unintelligible.

Today, for example, I dwell in the post-memory of illness. Nothing cataclysmic–just a knock-down, drag-out body-wracked-with-fever flu. Powerful enough, though, to take me to that retreating vantage from which all of the day's other sails seem distant, the horizon unfamiliar, the body bobbing in a space of uncanny solitude. Call it my own "meshes of the afternoon," because whole days figure like dreamspace when sickness hails this way, and certain childhood memories wrap me, warp me unexpectedly into a curve of time I must need to dwell in to get well.

Can any of us have enough patience with this process, so resistant to being shaken out of our familiar routine, to being, only temporarily, we hope, dropped from the timetables? And how is my being here, in a space alongside of, merely prepositional in every way, without a referent, how is this so different from the place from which I write? There is this question about writing: whether with each transmutation of the self into syntax I am writing myself into or out of time, at least out-of-time as we know it; whether I wish to ally myself with the known or belie it; whether I wish to insert myself into a sentence or be carried away by it. I know there is a role played by randomness in the work of re-imagining reality that is the process of forcing sentences onto a page, forging images out of words. Randomness and interruptives. Like this illness that's come upon me just as I was poised to compose a difficult passage into the portrait of a friendship I am trying to represent–a friendship between a gay man and a lesbian–a friendship and enmity and the whole difficult mix of trying to nurture one another or to read beyond our own habits of self-destruction for a voice we can love and recognize. As much as I try to invite the randomness or control it, there are these interruptions. But what I come to see is that they are part of the writing too. To be poised outside of a doorway: will it eventually take me back to the room in which I write?

After two days of reluctant caretaking–it's not that my lover doesn't love me, but that illness makes her angry because it reminds her of death–Jean has a nightmare that she has to "nurse" a baby, but her breasts are too small and the baby is undernourished. Just two days out of commission, but I feel I've been out of "life" forever, and it's not clear I'll be able to return. (A friend tells me it's an (ex-)Catholic thing–all those stories of ailing martyrs tinge even the most routine illness with high drama and the hope or fear of eternal life.)

Perhaps that is when memories come–when you feel as though your place in time is coming undone. Or maybe it's less pressingly ontological, and more fundamentally sensual: you remember because you hear the sound of voices in the outer room the way you did as a child; you remember because the feeling of a blanket pulled to the warm, dark core of your neck, of your breathing, will always make you remember. It's one of those gestures that brings you into being every time it is carried out, and therefore brings you back. You pull the coverlet over yourself now, or your lover does it for you, and you love the way the new sheet feels at first cool on your warm skin, and you love the way she lifts it from two corners to waft over you like a sail. But someone else did it then. No, not a father. Never, certainly, a father's hands, *like curtains of fright his hands pull that darkness over your eyes with every slap.* But it *is* my father I'm remembering now, and possibly his love.

Illness forces me to sleep during the day and wake at odd hours of the night, and it is then that the door opens onto a remembered scene of folding and enfolding, of being held in the furtive manufacture of a gift. It wasn't something that happened with my father often if at all. The door has opened onto a dusk-lit, post-dinner scene involving stiff brown construction paper–an industrial variety of generic drafting board that my father brings home from work expressly for this project. There is a geometry aloft, a soft lead pencil is required, a straight arm. My father applies himself to it. For me. The cardboard is smooth as a blanket. Am I sick? Is that what has inspired this act of out-of-the-blue concern? I'm both groggy and excited and conjoined–how *will* the block of paper transform into a tepee for my doll?

I wasn't one for dolls, *ever,* but I latched onto this doll of a girl "Indian" late in life. I was probably already on the cusp of adolescence when I took to this doll and tried through her to regress to a space of caretaking play with my father.

Now I was remembering the glittery atmosphere from which she hailed, her campy origin. We hardly ever ate out, not only because my father's slim salary didn't allow it but because, to understate the case, my father had trouble with food. Food didn't like him, one might conclude. (He wasn't, after all, a tremendously likable guy.) Everything had to be bland; something was bound to upset his stomach. "Oh, no, I can't eat that," he'd say to every sumptuous or succulent offering: "I'll be on the toilet for days." So I can't say what it was about the Longhorn Restaurant that beckoned my father to leave his ailing body for one night, every now and again, and give himself over to sirloins (well-done) with spicy barbecue sauce. The Longhorn Family Restaurant, I only know, stands tall as its high-hatted cowboys in my memory for F-U-N in neon letters. For a singular mutual glow, all around. "Well, what'll ya have, little Lady?" a waitress bursting at the seams of her turquoise satin wranglers sidles up to me to ask. Her name tag is "Buffalo Bill Cody." She's a woman; she's a man. I'm mesmerized. My name-tag, because we got them too, is "Billy the

Kid." My father is laughing and eating, and eating and laughing. And who can tell how or why this restaurant with its Western motif, so unlike home in the Northeastern United States, sets wheels spinning inside my father's eyes that say he has a need that can be met and even nourished. It must be kitsch, I decide as an adult. My father had a queer side that had been driven underground. A South Philly guy, my father pictured his neighborhood for us in stories of broken limbs, and blinding accidents where there should have been fireworks, and the random violences of petty Mafia. No corner was safe in his world. But he differentiated himself by way of a penchant for country western songs and yodellers and the sentimental plunk of a sad guitar. My mother read his predilection for "Opry" over "Opera" as another sign of his lack of culture, a signifier of an unschooled background, an impoverishment of taste. Or perhaps she could tell the forms that moved him, that made him well, had all the earmarks of drag.

That evening I chose the Indian doll from a display case near the cash register–was it somebody's birthday? Maybe my own? She was slender and my age and meant as a "collectable," but I wished to treat her as a doll whose limbs could bend to follow the paths of some earlier, important interrupted dream. To take me there. And my father seems captivated too. He's assembling a home for her on our dining room table, and asking me, *please do,* to inscribe pictures on her tepee's walls. I'm too old for this, and I know it, but next thing, I'm lying belly to rug in the living room, studying the terrain, lolling before a story that will unwind for me and my doll. The tepee is about two feet tall but the diameter of its base is too narrow for me to see clearly or with enough light what the doll is doing once she's gone inside. But I'm trying to make it work, playing on the rug in the light of my father's gaze, trained on the television set, his mouth, a grimace, he bites his nails to a pulp. "Can we, can we keep wandering into a field of grace?" the memory seems to inquire, the sick woman turned child wants to know.

But these days rapt by fever aren't all so determinedly elegiac. There are moments, for example, of feminist disgust when, as through a veil, I glimpse an episode on TV of Marilyn Monroe clad now in a sweater and tights, now in a bathing suit. Everyone else in the film wears three-piece suits, not a fleck of flesh exposed. Her nakedness so vulnerably, garishly out of place. She's singing "My Heart Belongs to Daddy," no doubt intended by Cole Porter to be sung between man and man or man and boy, but here she's pouting the lyrics into a lock of mussed hair while a gaggle of men tosses her around the room of what could be a bachelor fraternity party. "It's making me sick to watch this," I tell my queer friend, Jim. "Yes, she looks so baffled in that film as though she's wondering what she's doing there," he observes. Why would I want to return to *this* land of the living? Hollywood can be so *unheimlich*. But there are moments of queer celebration, too, that, lucky for me, rise before the proscenium of my illness. The credits appear, still through a filmy gaze, for *Easter Parade* with Judy Garland and Fred Astaire. How is it I could have never seen this film? The muscles in my face move to make a smile that lasts for a full two hours, and even tears. Brown slacks, velvet pumps, white plumage; turquoise diamond blouses, yellow flounces, red plumage. Hats, hats and hats. A parody of Fred and Ginger, a tap dance to beat the band. A gay man and a lesbian out for a drive or a stroll down the boulevard. Usually Fred is the one I watch, but here Judy steals the show. How is it I had never recognized until now Judy Garland's dykiness? A sexual persona quite distinct perhaps from her personification as a gay male icon. It's a tough girl edge melded with a charming softness; it's a range of affect from serious lover to clown, from a woman who believes in her words to a woman who can parody them in an instant. "Musicals make everybody queer," Jim says, and I start to yearn for a contemporary musical, and I begin to consider how one instance of a queer aesthetic does more for queer self-representation than all the transparent stories of our lives could ever do.

Perceptions contract and mutate while I'm ill. I can't move my upper torso for stomach cramps, as though the rubber soled heel of the foot of a giant were grinding into my abdomen. I try to paddle across water with a float lodged beneath my stomach to ease the pain. I'm literally losing my guts. My head, so wrapped in the proverbial Woolfian cotton gauze, only has room for small thoughts. My dreams happen in claustrophobic crawlspaces; this afternoon for instance, the light like charcoal, I have a dream that is the sensation of a weird attack: my father is thwacking the backs of my mother's and my bra straps. When the rubber snaps and pinches against my back, I say, "That's not nice. That's not a nice thing to do," I tell him. I really can't be this cold for very long. How does a fever know how or when or how high to climb? The heat through my lips feels euphoric. My clothes drenched with sweat will have to be changed if I don't want the cold to return. This afternoon's movie, nevertheless–and when *do* I ever watch a movie of an afternoon?–has struck my head like a faith healer and when I next look up it's into the color of natural food dyes: I'm looking through a canary yellow, pelican orange, now pink, now green, a confectioner's purple window. With what confidence the color adheres to the grain of an egg's chalky surface, those same colors yielding to the grain of the film. It's all I have energy for right now. I read the directions, addressed to a six-year-old, slowly. I move, arrange, eggs in water to boil, dip, wait and watch. I'm definitely getting better.

Next day, alone in our small garden, I rake the debris that winter has tucked into its edges. I make way for blooms. Bugs come in all shapes, furs and shells, glistening, an earthworm turns, out of the ground. I pull two plastic chairs to the center of a square of bricks I've just cleared, and sit, lie, looking up. High up, higher than the naked eye can reach, I glimpse a kite caught in a branch, its tail, flapping in a mighty high-blowing wind. Kites figure powerfully for me, ever since I took one to an abandoned lot as a child, up while everyone else was sleeping. The kite was strung with fishing wire, and the wind pulled it so high, I could barely discern its true shape, weight, depth, or size. Tiny and taut as a bird. I almost feared being uplifted myself, but I held my own ground-ward and worked with the wind. An older boy wandered by: "I've never seen a kite go up that high." And I held on for dear life until the kite descended with a crazy swirl and thump into a tree. Is it really a kite, I begin to wonder, or more likely a plastic bag, so many pieces of trash impaled on trees like artificial leaves that I'm glancing this morning? "Yeah, it's just a trash bag caught in the branches . . ." It's akin, this dichotomy–sentimental kite or materialist trash–to the dilemma I've been grappling with in the work of my most recent writing. I'm trying to represent a beloved other, and I move between idealizing him and making him so real he is repugnant. This morning, I'm all eyes, until I consider the effects of a too high premium placed on visuality. I have to return to my body, I think, if I'm going to return to my writing desk, not just re-gain my eyes. Perception isn't reducible to what we see but to a polymorphously perverse body. Give me a poetry of the toe. A fiction wrought by hand. And the stomach, my god, the stomach. Where else does my writing come from if not from there?

I prick up my ears. There are voices.

The sentiments of a favorite slender volume on the practice of reading by Lynne Sharon Schwartz echo far and wide in me. *"For here is the essence of true reading: learning to live in another's voice, to speak another's language. . . . [Reading] is escape from the boundaries of our own voices and idioms. . . . From Faulkner to Gertrude Stein to Virginia Woolf, the writers who claim our attention do so by voice and idiom, which are the audible manifestations of the mind. This is how it sounds inside, they declare. Listen, hear the shape with me. There is good reason for the addictive cravings of readers: the only new thing under the sun is the sound of another voice."* Kids pound hoops in the alleyway under night lights; bats flutter, unnoticed above them, as I write this; airplanes tunnel through the sky overhead; laughter and screams waft up, like bits of dreams broken off from their bodies. Amid the layers of interdependent night life and day life, the comings and goings, the complex motion, is it voices that abide? Does the voice inhere? What is fulfilled in listening to the sound of one's own writing? Like listening to the sound of one's breathing? Are they the same? Or is one's writing better said in the voice of another, the real pleasure in hearing it read back to one?

I'm in an airplane travelling from Vancouver to Chicago to Providence. Better not to know how long the journey will be. Just endure it. So I begin by piling into my lap my self-made first-aid kit of reading, writing and music. Today I want to be in the sound of two of my favorite gay New York school poets–James Schuyler and Frank O'Hara. Schuyler for his Zen master purity of line. O'Hara for the sound of ecstatic talking he brings off, outmoded joy. I'm reading another gay writer, Edmund White, on James Schuyler, quoting a poem about the merits of observation over simple revelation, self-expression:

> "'Your poems,'
> a clunkhead said, 'have grown
> more open.' I don't want to be open,
> merely to say, to see and say, things
> as they are."

A light flicks on, like the kind and silent opening of a shade. How nice, I think, the steward, quiet as a librarian, has tucked me into my books for the journey. Now I chuckle and nod before a poem by O'Hara:

Anxiety

I'm having a real day of it.
                                   There was
something I had to do. But what?
There are no alternatives, just
the one something.
                          I have a drink,
it doesn't help–far from it!
                                         I
feel worse. I can't remember how
I felt, so perhaps I feel better.
No. Just a little darker.
                                If I could
get really dark, richly dark, like
being drunk, that's the best that's
open as a field. Not the best,

but the best except for the impossible
pure light, to be as if above a vast
prairie, rushing and pausing over
the tiny golden heads in deep grass.
But still now, familiar laughter low
from a dark face, affection human and often even–

motivational? the warm walking night
                                   wandering
amusement of darkness, lips,
                             and
the light, always in wind. Perhaps
that's it: to clean something. A window?

I'm struck by the play on "openness" by both writers–Schuyler eschewing it for its naivete, O'Hara celebrating it as recuperative like the cleaning of a window. It reminds me of my own tug-of-war between an interest in devising, indulging, looking out for, imitating a *queer aesthetic* over and against a representational impulse (a synonym for mere openness?). Is it our charge as gay writers to hold a mirror up to our experience (so often such narratives change nothing but succeed in flattening our lives), or to find the form that will answer to queer habits of being, radical sensibilities and ideologies? To begin with a self-consciously chosen discourse of the self by way of autobiography rather than the see-through swatch of "experience." Instead of setting out to tell the transparent story of her life–no life is see-through and language is anything but clear–a queer memoirist could begin with the axiom, prayer, conversation, the childhood fable, game, collection, or song, a recipe, a mental jingle, a set of instructions and to let that odd byway determine the form her remembering will take. To try to write the story that is so close to her skin she cannot see it to read. I'm wondering how I can make this happen in the project I'm in the middle of on queer friendship (between gay men and lesbians) when the voice of an older male passenger seated beside me interrupts me. It happens to me all the time in public, shared, or confined spaces with men. At the local YMCA, for example, where I'm trying desperately to experience meditative exercise. Even though I can barely see through my goggles and I'm wearing earplugs, the elderly men at the pool, and they alone, address me, talking me up as though I'm seated next to them at a straight singles bar, longing for their company. I point to my earplugs, and yell, "I can't hear you!" The stories they want to tell only bounce off the water with more force and volume. This doesn't happen to Jean. We're at the same pool, same time, same men, but it is me whom they ask: "Why aren't you working?" "How many students *are* there where you teach?" "Your breaststroke is good but would you like some tips on your backstroke? As for the freestyle, bring your left hand into the water thumbward and brush your hand against your hip as though you're taking change out of your hip pocket." It's as though, to their eyes, I exist as their hearer bearers. I exist to be told. My face can be trained downward, now I'm going under, across the pool, but the chatter continues. "Well, it doesn't happen to *me*," Jean says, as though it's something that I do, a way, that invites strange men to talk to me, unasked and uninvited. It's true I'm interested in other people's stories, and I read for the sound of another's voice, but theirs? I can't remember how it starts this time. I *was* buried in my books, wasn't I? After an hour's worth of conversation passes between myself and the person seated next to me, I glance across the aisle for a glimpse of Jean. She's sandwiched between two men, not a word has passed between them while she applies unbroken concentration to her papers.

Maybe the thinness of my boundaries–my Italian/American family was one billowing, immense body of amorphous libido in which everyone was holding on for dear life to every other one and no differences could be discerned–showed on my face. Is that what openness meant? Maybe I was perceived as open, which, where women are concerned, too often means non-existent. The man sitting next to me is a high-ranking official at a major research university. He addresses me as though we've been made to share a bunk at bootcamp. The tone of his question suggests we're going to be together for a very long time, so we may as well get to know one another. Which doesn't mean he initiates this conversation grudgingly or without (a brand of male administrational) enthusiasm. His university has just hired a literary theorist as Dean, so he asks me to explain "deconstruction." I answer as though I'm in a job interview, but I come out to him too. This doesn't staunch the flow of the conversation. Peering out the window from time to time, he announces that the plane has taken an inexplicable turn North. He's nervous. That's why he wants the company of my voice, and I begin to believe that anything is possible on an airplane, maybe even real conversation–the goal of writing–because flying throws people together in mutual distress, above ground; voices break through in liminal space. I become more animated, open to the possibility, but instead our colloquy takes a nose-dive. He's doing what Americans, and especially high-ranking ones, love to do. He's venturing "opinions." About African-Americans–whose women, defiantly superhuman, over-protect their men; about working class people–who are worse bigots than he, who represent a Darwinian (he's a scientist) common denominator; about feminists–don't you think they are *making* men beastly, by denigrating them? Men really don't act that way. I try, via my working class background and feminist education, to challenge and re-work every point he makes. I'm disagreeing pretty strongly, but I'm also aware that I'm locked into the seat next to him, that I literally can't exit the conversation if it becomes too contentious. But he's smiling too much to convince me that he's heard my voice, smiling smugly as if to say ain't it great to be an American where you can sit on an airplane and make pronouncements about groups of people in the form of idle chit chat and still feel as though it's an exchange of ideas you're having because you are smarter than the rest and, well, life is grand, and this talk with this little lady here, and she's an "intelligent woman," I have to say, it all makes me feel a little less anxious and a little gladder to be alive.

Are we being open with one another, me and my friend, an educated version of the status quo, or am I merely responding to the call of a father's voice?

It must be his father-figurelyness that keeps me engaged. My book on friendship between lesbians and gay men makes me want to understand how I transformed, in my adult friendships with gay men, the void that was the conversation that never happened between my father and me, the silence that inheres in so many father/daughter relations. I told him, partly erroneously, that my book was about friendships (by which I meant the possibility for conversation and identification) between men and women–I didn't say between queer men and women.

As the plane begins its descent, he asks me what gives me the most pleasure, what makes me happiest about writing. And he claims to want to know why I write, what I hope for someone else to "get" out of my writing. I talk about the work of writing and the risks of writing, and about the difficulty and desire to achieve beauty and grace in an ugly world, not a beauty that would allow us to escape the ugliness, I try to explain, but a disruptive beauty. An interruptive beauty. A beauty that requires confrontation. He wants to write too, it turns out, the story of what it has been like for him to lose his mother to Alzheimer's disease. His mother was a realist painter of the order of Andrew Wyeth and he wants to understand what it might have been like for her to lose hold of the preciseness of that world. He wants, I'm sure, to understand his loss.

As the plane begins its descent, he talks about his body. He's marveling again at the cellular complexity that forms ligaments that move the fingers in his hand. He tells me he is recently preoccupied with the physiology of hearing, what changes occur in the brain to make hearing happen. I ask him if he thinks that vision and hearing are interdependent because I recently took a test that showed I had a visually oriented brain when I think of myself as more aurally attuned. I told him, in all sincerity, of how as a writer, I interpret this question of the physiology of hearing in terms of the idea of a voice. That what writers make is voices. That what compels me like a mystery about writing is how its voice, any voice, is essentially there, a sign of life, and supremely intangible. I ask him if he's ever happened upon the voice of a deceased loved one on a tape recorder after they've died, and how the sound, timbre, weight, buoyancy, staccato, or depth or hesitancy, the sound of the voice brings you into indisputable, painfully intimate contact with their being in a way that photographic reproduction never could. We talk about voices, and how I hear them as hallmarks of being. He says he's never thought of it that way. He seems honestly intrigued. And then he says, in spite of the fact that he has the one seat on the plane that happens not to have a seat in front of it, he says, his legs outstretched, he's feeling cramped. "How can you feel cramped?!" I practically yell.

De-planing, I make a brusque and tired good-bye. I've got to find that 1970s Barbara Hammer film and watch it again, I think, the one with the exploding vulvic flowers, to help me better understand the disruptive beauty I say I want my work to be about. De-planing, I return to the thought that I was leaning toward that he had interrupted: I had started to feel unsettled by the way darkness was figuring in O'Hara's poem. How could it not be racialized, merely a trope for his own disrupture from himself? Perhaps O'Hara was using darkness in the same way I'd as a child used the "Indian." To quell my own darkness, to attach desire to the dark Other as vehicle. Maybe the conversation with this man quelled his darkness, but it didn't change anything. Writing had to be about something more than the acquisition (as of an object) of joy. If I'm going to write queerly, I need to know what I'm in conversation with.

A man clothed in a frock sits on the other side of the door. He must be kindly, he must be bold. They have led you to believe he is worthy. What most matters to you is that he not be clammy. For it's the image of a skullcap that you can't shake when you picture him, and a brooding brow. His hair you'd prefer to think is parted on the side like a boy's. His fingers you'd like to believe are slender as lily stems, not the sweaty palms or wide maw that alarms you with its pointing, with the direction it could insist upon you–"There, there, go there," it points, but you don't want to go there so it slithers like a snake to bite you out from behind a picket fence.

Who is he, the man who hears my child whispers in the dark, to whom I give the core of me, a newly, freshly lit wick, my untouched flame? What odd concoctions does the husky voice of an eight year old fabricate for an old man's delectation in the dark?

This week I have learned the word "fancy," and I show my love for it by anointing everything with its name–the lettuce is fancy; I should like to have a fancy candy; he is a fancy clown; the snowfall, a tooth, my mother's hands–everything can be this word if I want it: fancy ice, pearls, mama. Fancy mother. Fancy mama. Fancy mama face in the mirror smile at me. Today all I know is the tassel on my red shoes that has been studying me; an itch where my soft curls are caught in the back of my collar; a running hee-hee-hee, high-pitched, who can suck their air in and hold it and then scream? in the schoolyard. I kiss my girlfriend, a peck, and don't hide my eyes. Today I know gum in a white green packet with a red stripe and a few numbers and the word "fancy." But you have learned me a prayer and you would like more from me. You would like me to find a bruise on the back of my hand where there is none. I have nothing to roll around in my mouth, no gum or candy is allowed in here, nothing to remind me that I have a body. "Fancy," I sigh, waiting for you waiting for me. You open the sliding window to my voice. You wait daily for the children to speak to you, to breathe warmly, directly into your ear even when their breath smells of tomato soup and sleep because this dark room makes them sleepy. I can't see you but I'll talk anyway; I'll say the prayer and count sins as if to edge them deep into the wood with a bowie knife so I can finger them when I've returned and own them–these things you've told me to say, these things you want to make of me. If I told you color, would that count? The color of my father's work clothes, blue-gray, scares me, and a soily metallic smell and the hard knob of his boot. I feel better when my mother lifts the pink comb and strokes my hair. After dinner, I lay my head in her lap for what seems like hours. I would like to glue flowers into my notebook to save them or else they'll die. I would also like to eat them. I would rather suck on my sock than eat peas. I should like not to trip when I run home from school when I'm forced to wink at sun or rain. I would like someone to hold my hand then. But all you want to know is that I smacked my doll, hard, twice. This I did. That I lied and stole and wished my father dead. But I didn't lie or steal though I shall try to in future so as to have something to tell you in my boomerang voice. And I shouldn't have couldn't have known yet that I wished my father dead. I didn't not love him yet, I didn't love him yet to know that. So how about you? What you gonna say? You stinky sock man on the other side of the door? I made that up. Because I don't think I like you. Your voice smells like "tap-rooms," that's what my fancy mama calls them, or an ink-well, and sometimes salad dressing.

"Please bless me father and I have offended thee," my voice says, is allowed to say. And yours says, say this, do that. "I know you'll be back," yours says, "because sin is original and unchanging, you'll circle back to me, waiting to make you more and more mine with each return, to hear me tell you again that you were bad and I will remain here, a voice with a bad body, and you can't see me. And you will spend your whole life saying what I told you to say and listening for a different reply from me."

"And I will spend the better part of my life," I say, "trying to remember what I would have said if I could and starting over from there. And you will have to intone something other than penance in your voice on the other side of the door lest it crack, wither, and die."

I am a lesbian. I am a writer. Is it possible to utter those sentences without re-entering the confessional, for even if a writer, as a woman, I am a thief; I take an authority not freely given. For queer self-representation to have political force, to change the body politic, it needs to stop addressing itself to doctors and priests. But that isn't something it does anymore, you say. Our writing is addressed to queer audiences, liberating constituencies, gender outlaws, activist communities, and it comes in an array of genres and critiques. Until we examine the political unconscious operating in our work, I won't be convinced that the confessional, white male father figure and all, doesn't continue to play a major authorizing role.

Memories, dreams, cinematographs are my templates because they augur an unconscious, and a political unconscious at that. Father nurture, colored eggs, an ethic of care of the self; odd intrusions, reparation, surplus of meaning. I think that all of those things figure in the illness I described at the outset because of the writing I am currently trying to do. The imagery brought to bear into or out of the well of my recent sickness was dictated in part by the writing I'm trying and failing to do, but it, that imagery, seemingly unbidden, will also return me to my writing via a new path.

One part of a portrait of my gay friend Wally has kept me poised on the edge of doubt, unwilling to write for a very long time. It's the matter of alcoholism, and my desire to find Wally via my representation in something other than the garb of *the* drunk, *the* addict. The recent knowledge that the identity categories "homosexual" and "addict" were contemporaneous late 19th century inventions makes me even more reluctant to figure my friend *as* alcoholic (Sedgwick). The consolidation of a set of practices into an identity as such did no favors for either set of persons, especially when doctors could claim homosexuals were addicted to sex and thus saddle us with a double aberration. I mine the thesaurus whole afternoons for synonyms for "drunk" as both noun (indeed, subject) and adjective because I want to know how Wally would wear any of those designations, just as I seek out the form for myself: "teetotaler." This was something my father called himself, and I begin to realize an identification with my otherwise silent, absent, uncaring, and hard to care for father. The dreams and memories where my father suddenly figures for me have everything to do with my trying to make sense of my caring for Wally and his caring for me. It's not that there's a one-to-one correspondence between the people we love, or failed to, past and present, but that past narratives, remembered scenarios, current dreams tell us what we didn't know about the past and fail to know about the present. I conjure those in order to better speak their languages or more fully realize how their language speaks me.

As lesbians, we are displaced, whether ill or well; we inhabit the world with a difference. It's that space I exploit in order to better know it when I write; it's that space I seek to make real with each newly imagined conviction of it.

I close this writing to begin again. I return to my writing desk beckoned by the voices in the outer room. Are the lights off or on? Is the body coiled or extended? Is the ground close at hand or a plummeting descent? Hushed or exuberant, their silences as real as their murmurs, the voices of other lives subsist in an outer room. It might be the voice of my mother trundling like a sewing machine across a textured surface. It might be the voice of my father, yelling, grunting, breaking. Or the cavernous voice of a newscaster, the high pitched laugh of a visiting friend, the repeated clucking of a child tongue against its palette. It might be one side of a long and winding story told into a telephone receiver, the climbing, the tremolo of the soprano who lives next door, the banal chuckle of the salesman at the door, "al-righty," you can sense the sweet smell of his aftershave. It is Aunt Francis' voice from whom everything was taken too soon, robbed, her voice was thin; it's grandmother Rose's robust cackle; the rise and fall to emphasis of Uncle Joe's latest joke. It might be Aunt Josephine's whose voice was sped up since the death of her daughter, or Sister Mary Conrad's stern command. The voices are even as when affect is flattened by dark news and the movement of acts that must be carried out. Arrangements. The voices are forgetful of themselves, loose-tongued, and gay, clanking of party-goers. The voices are desperate whispers punctuated by sighs, punctuated by sobs. The voices speak of a person in an inner room, with hope or care; the voices have forgotten the person in the inner room, without regret, unaware. The voices are inconsequential, and profoundly there. You only imagine the scent of rose water, or an encroaching blue light, when all that is real is these voices, their necessary but meaningless utterance. These voices can never go where you are going, or come to your calling. Their nature is to remain on the other side of the door.

You write to remember their comfort. You write to give them bodies. You write to understand how they suspend your body in solitude or pain. You write so they will hear you. You write to be among them, or in spite of them. You write because it is the tone of desire that is the salve. You write because the tone has not been struck, has not been heard, of this desire. And tone is everything. You write to coax your own voice, your own listening. You write because you must pretend to know what they were saying while you were gone. You write because you don't want to be afraid of saying what the voices would tell you if they could, or what you would tell them. You write to check the impulse to tell them to stop making so much noise, because their din is too much, you write in reply to their comforting discomfort. You write because there is always an absent one among the many whose voice you crane to hear. Because the sound of a voice is better than the sound of a second-hand ticking in an empty room. In the hour of my need, I know that I will want the voice of my lover to sing to me.

WORKS CITED

Allen, Donald, ed. *The Selected Poems of Frank O'Hara*. NY: Vintage Books, 1974. 117-118.

Schwartz, Lynne Sharon. *Ruined by Reading: A Life in Books*. Boston: Beacon Press, 1996.

Sedgwick, Eve Kosofsky. "Epidemics of the Will." *Tendencies*. Durham: Duke University Press, 1993. 130-142.

White, Edmund. *The Burning Library: Essays*. New York: Alfred A. Knopf, 1994.

k/not theory: a self-dialogue

Maya Chowdhry

SUMMARY. This paper discusses the role of the personal experience in the writing process. Using a personal/journal writing style the author charts the journey of a recent play *Skin into Rainbows* from first draft to production. The author plays with the constructs of writing and juxtapositions these against a form of Knot Theory to measure their value, playing with math and language techniques in a search for truth. *[Article copies available for a fee from The Haworth Document Delivery Service: 1-800-342-9678. E-mail address: <getinfo@haworthpressinc.com> Website: <http://www.HaworthPress.com>]*

KEYWORDS. Self-writing, racism, identity, lesbians, poetry

Maya Chowdhry, MA, is an award winning playwright, poet, writer and inTeraCt-ive Artist. Her plays include: *Skin into Rainbows* (Theatre Centre National Tour, 1999), *Seeing* (workshopped at The Royal Court Theatre, 1999), *Kaahini* (tours by Birmingham Repertory Company, 1998, and Red Ladder Theatre Company, 1997– nominated for The Writers' Guild Best Children's Theatre Award), *An Appetite for Living* (West Yorkshire Playhouse, 1997), *Taking the Rap* (Oldham Theatre Workshop, 1997), *Splinters* (Bradford Theatre in the Mill, 1997, and Talawa Theatre at The Lyric Studio, 1998). She has written five plays for BBC radio including *Monsoon* (1991). *Monsoon*, a winner in the 1991 BBC Young Playwrights Festival, was nominated for the 1993 BBC Newcomers Award at the Prix Futura in Berlin and published in *Six Plays by Black and Asian Women Writers* (Aurora Metro Publications, 1991). In 1994 she was Resident Dramatist with Red Ladder Theatre Company and from 1991 to 1994 she was a member of the editorial collective of Feminist Arts News. Her poetry has been published in: *Healing Strategies for Women at War: seven black women poets*, *As Girls Could Boast* and other anthogies. It is collected in *Putting in the Pickle Where the Jam Should Be and Climbing Mountains* (audio). She won the 1992 Cardiff International Poetry competition with *Brides of Dust*.

Address correspondence to: Maya Chowdhry, 18 Vickers Road, Firth Park, Sheffield S5 6UZ UK (e-mail: MayaChowdhry@inventingreality.freeserve.co.uk).

[Haworth co-indexing entry note]: "k/not theory: a self-dialogue." Chowdhry, Maya. Co-published simultaneously in *Journal of Lesbian Studies* (Harrington Park Press, an imprint of The Haworth Press, Inc.) Vol. 4, No. 4, 2000, pp. 59-70; and: *Lesbian Self-Writing: The Embodiment of Experience* (ed: Lynda Hall) Harrington Park Press, an imprint of The Haworth Press, Inc., 2000, pp. 59-70. Single or multiple copies of this article are available for a fee from The Haworth Document Delivery Service [1-800-342-9678, 9:00 a.m. - 5:00 p.m. (EST). E-mail address: getinfo@haworthpressinc.com].

Maya Chowdhry
Photo by Seni Seneviratne. Used by permission.

<u>january nineteen ninety nine:</u>
i, not I.
I. not. i?
i . . . not?
knots?
where.
can.
i?
find a pronoun?
(we, their, this, ourselves)
second person impersonal.
begin again with she.

but what about the gender defiance?
s/he. s(he).

the page begins to fill up with forward slashes /
s(he) uses them in her play texts to denote an interruption
by another character. s(he) interrupts herself constantly. uses
brackets and italics to denote actions, (*emotions*). does k/not finish
sentences, uses . . . when the words run out, when s(he) can k/not
bear to write the unthinkable. none of this is for *emphasis* /

s(he) looks for a theory for the k/nots
in her life and buries herself in maths[1],
in the scientific discovery of *(life)*.
s(he) will k/not fall . . .
it does k/not work because s(he) knows
what the dots re-present.

july nineteen ninety eight:
i visit the *(past)*. I am writing a play about separation[2], drawing on
Empedocles[3] theory, needing to find a way to unify the disparate
elements in my life. the theatre company i have been commissioned by
wants a play with an Asian story; i say 'mixed-race' and then get lost
in the labels/theories of identities. i do k/not get as far as sexuality.

3:00 am i trawl the world wide web inputting 'mixed-race' - it brings
up a load of personals from 'white' seeking 'black': so identity is
about who you want to sleep with? i keep coming back to personal
history, baulking and inputting another search item. i redefine my
search, come back to experience, to an eleven year old girl with long
hair in plaits that continually get pulled in the school playground.

this was not play.

i want to honour my writing process but i battle with the memories, the
war at home, the escape to my grandparents' home, the confusion and
pain of that growing up.

write it down. change it. move on.

move on from the memories.

i trawl my 'how-to' writing books, read a chapter from *'Writing for Your Life'*, do an exercise from *'Writing from the Heart'* and finally go to bed, only to complete an exercise on objectivity from *'How to Write While You Sleep . . .'*

i decide to set the play in the future; it feels safe, distant. it is after the identity wars; the new human race is genetically engineered to be orange; feelings are tightly controlled; the world is tightly controlled: the world is Ocean Floor a large dome under the sea that now covers the whole of planet earth; there are no elements; there are no mothers, only care-consultants; everyone is born from an embryo bank and lives in dwellings, alone, controlled by Dwelling Consoles.

safety.

no way of getting hurt.

the eleven year old main character, Kumkum, has a dream, perceives her difference, sets out on a 'virtual-reality[4] memory-field' excursion to uncover why she's different. she travels to the past looking for herself and discovers her family, her birth-mother, connections with ancestry. the mother is intuitive, in her visions she reaches out for Kumkum, tries to help her with her questions. Kumkum reaches out to the past that she has been told does not exist, looks for an answer to who she is. she discovers a lost embryo with a destiny that involves being frozen for fifty one years.

Kumkum arrives in the past (1999) on a Virtual-Reality Memory-Field excursion)) and asks:

KUMKUM: Is this world in the present or past of time?
SAMEER: Not my past.
KUMKUM: Is it mine?
SAMEER: I do not know, I do not know you, I have only met you
today and today is my present.

it is just before Kumkum's birthing-day and the only *present* she wants
is an answer to her questions about who she is . . .

in the *reality of* my world the theatre company asks me to change the
title; there are problems with it, the connotations of 'separation' -
divorce. divorce from what I ponder and then get lost in a sea of words
searching for a new title. i decide that *'Separation'* is probably too
naive a title, even through Empedocles theory of separation and unification makes so much sense to me in the here and now. then why
does it k/not work in practice?

because we do k/not live in our heads; we live out there in the world,
in the world(s).

somehow I visit the worlds or the worlds visit me and I shape and
sculpt and tell *(lies)* until the first draft of the play is written.

february nineteen ninety nine:
s(he) blocks, freezes, goes in on herself, escapes in her world and s(he)
can k/not find a way through. s(he) is in *(turmoil),* misses deadlines.
finally makes it: writes (rights?) the second draft. s(he) changes the
title of the play to *'Skin into Rainbows'* and suddenly a whole world
opens up that s(he) could k/not see, and s(he) realises that all the
characters see more clearly than s(he) does:

SAMEER: Live for today.
DOLLY: And tomorrow will take care of itself.

in the space between finishing the second draft and waiting for feedback s(he) reviews her Art Therapy, discovers a chalk sketch of the bottom of the sea in an old notebook. the *play* was there all the time, just biding its time. at the beginning of the play:

ZUHRAH: Time for virtual-learning-day, do not forget to nutrient yourself.
KUMKUM: What is time?
ZUHRAH: The indefinite continued progress of existence, events etc. in past, present, and future regarded as a whole. Now begin.

but this dialogue does k/not make it into the production script - the definition of time is edited out because it is the writer's (thoughts), not the character's.

march nineteen ninety nine:
my work is published in an anthology of Black[5] women's poetry - *'Healing Strategies for Women at War: seven black women poets'.* the publishers want me to read/perform at the launch. i have k/not performed for five years. i tell them i have stopped performing because i was dying, they do k/not take me literally and still try to persuade me. i finally agree but do not read the title poem - speaking my (own truth) aloud has become too *real*:

Healing Strategies for Women at War

one, leave knives on the chopping board
two, fry your love in hot oil
until it reaches flash point
three, stir yourself up
with therapy books on anger,
pinch yourself to see if you're still alive
four, lay the table with friends
placing them carefully, separate
with napkins, knives, forks and spoons

five, cut yourself into thin slices,
six, bake your dreams until
they carbonise in the oven
seven, stew family photographs, remember
comparisons and memories should be kept secret
eight, feed your addictions with the guilt
of using broken biscuits as a base for your life
nine, sprinkle: don't talk don't trust don't feel
into conversations about happiness
ten, devour the emotional distress
and wounds of others as your mirror
eleven, boil yourself in the pain of leaving
every time someone falls in love with you
twelve, ferment ginger wine kisses
until they burn your lips
thirteen, use pancakes garnished
with chillies to stuff your feelings into
fourteen, sift your desires through other's needs
fifteen, ice sex with pink fondant
and lie about what you want
sixteen, eat lotus root filled with miso
and pretend you're healthy
seventeen, make yourself
a packed lunch and leave home

i am faced with the poem and the play, although the play hints at a forbidden past the poem quite directly says "don't talk". i contemplate the nature of my poetic work which is challenging the forced amnesia of the society i am residing in.

the memory of the experience(s) comes into sharp focus and i return to theory to try to make sense of the emotions:

lines cross: "where two lines cross: we can't tell which strand is on top and which is on the bottom . . . much of Knot Theory[6] is done by considering the surface around the knot rather than the knot itself." s(he) scratches the surface with her writing, ties herself in knots trying to find a way through.

s(he) scratches her skin, first with her nails and then with a blade; it penetrates that breathing layer reaching into the depth of memory until a hidden story emerges. s(he) is wounded:

s(he) tries self-Shiatsu, homeopathy, flower essences, herbal essences, aromatherapy, crystal healing, feng shui and (*awakes)* one morning realising s(he) is a healing/theory junkie. s(he) tries intoxication: alcohol, one-night-stands, Internet sex, chat rooms and other forms of play and finally returns to the play. and when it is finished . . . /

april nineteen ninety nine:
there is a war going on: ethnic cleansing in europe and on our doorstep, 'white wolves' want to nail us to pavements to make us move out of our world. where shall we go to escape the hatred? the rehearsals go smoothly in a bomb-torn london, one on the doorstep in the east end. s(he) keeps rereading the millennium scene in the play:

KUMKUM: What if we're not here tomorrow, what if none of us are here?
DOLLY: What do you think is going to happen? We're in London on the eve of the Millennium, the turn of the century, of a new future and we're safe as houses.

s(he) doesn't feel safe in London, at home, in her world(s), s(he) wants to inhabit the play, live in Ocean Floor in 2064, after the identity wars of 2044. s(he) can't survive (*in the reality)* of the hatred.

at the end of the play:

ZUHRAH: If you feel different then be different.

how can s(he)?

s(he) does k/not know. s(he) returns to Empedocles: separation and unification, love and strife fracturing lives, tearing at the seams of a badly stitched multi-ethnic society.

can writing change the world? s(he) needs it to, to speak to the fragile minds of 9-11 year olds. s(he) is afraid: s(he) knows they know about difference but want to belong - are these mutually exclusive? s(he) is talking about skin colour very directly; is s(he) saying the unsayable?

s(he) stares at the end of the play for two weeks looking for an answer.

may nineteen ninety nine:
the actors do a line-run saying everything on the page, including the forward slashes and dots, they enjoy playing with the text, remembering the interruptions and unfinished sentences that have haunted them through the rehearsals.

the dress-rehearsal looms. they are real people but they are dressing up and acting. the play is about virtual reality - what is the reality of theatre? s(he), like Kumkum, has more questions than answers.

s(he) gets to the point in her life when s(he) does k/not want to live in the now. 'Herbal Highs' last one night and in the morning the mirror is steamed up and s(he) can k/not see if her eyes are still there. s(he) wonders because lately it feels like s(he) can k/not see anything.

s(he) begins on the page, begins again, has more endings and beginnings than a life can hold. s(he) thought that s(he) had let go of *'Skin into Rainbows'* but its torn edges wake her from the dream that tells her that nothing has changed.

did s(he) think a play could change her life, change her? her skin is brown not orange and s(he) could be dead from it, s(he) loves women and that could also get her killed, if s(he) does k/not get there first . . . "finish your sentences, do k/not leave truths half-told. spell it out." but s(he) gets her computer to do that. it crashes: k/not *enough* . . . memory.

s(he) meets a mathematician who shows her the equation for Knot Theory, but s(he) can k/not get both sides to balance. s(he) wonders why s(he) depends on experience to show her the meaning and re-solves to buy a book on mathematics, not pure maths but its applica-tions for relationships, for balance and equilibrium. s(he) makes a mental note to try an Internet *search* for *experience* perhaps 'Excite'.

the play goes on tour, s(he) lets go. gets involved in *'Dummy'* [7] a lesbian magazine and finds her-self in all her worlds at once.

s(he) goes to see the play in a school, sits in the back row, views from a safe distance. the audience does k/not know s(he)'s the writer (right-er?). s(he) does.

"the simplest knots are the unknot." which is not a knot. perhaps that's the answer. do k/not look for answers, only questions, do k/not look for imperatives only . . .

she does k/not know. s(he) needs a way through, a process to untie the k/nots.

s(he) uncovers Homeomorphism: " a continuous mapping between two spaces whose inverse is also continuous." s(he) considers spaces: the spaces between her worlds rather than the worlds that escape definition. s(he) decides that s(he) could live in the spaces in-between the lines on her page, in the spaces in-between writing and living, in the spaces s(he) does k/not feel s(he) has in her life. in the spaces between anything is possible: s(he) can be Black, queer . . . unlabeled . . . and her life begins to defy definition. does it?

points of safety:
i am lying?
constructs?
contracts?

k/not performing?
k/not inter-act-ing?
automythology?
truth?

all hypothesis must be testable - they must be susceptible, at least in principle, to being proven *wrong.*' [8]

(i decide *(based on experience))* that the process is k/not safe.

NOTES
1. Mathematics: the abstract science of number, quantity, and space studied in its own right (pure) or as applied to other disciplines such as physics, engineering, etc.

2. *Separation* (working title) finally became *Skin into Rainbows,* produced by Theatre Centre Limited for 9-11 year olds, their families and friends, national tour, 1999. There are a number of worlds in the play: dreamscape: dreams and psychic visions; virtual reality; the past; the present; the future; the possibility of a new future if events in the past are changed by a) time travel b) virtual time travel c) the influence of a vision that you perceived as any of the above.

3. Empedocles (495?-435 B.C.) was an early Greek philosopher. He became the first philosopher to argue that what exists can be reduced to four elements: air, earth, fire and water; he said that all other substances result from temporary combinations of these elements; the elements are eternal and unchanging, but their combining and separation appear as change. A force called love causes the elements to come together as compounds, and that a force called strife causes the compounds to break up. *(From IBM World Book CD-ROM)*

4. An image or environment generated by computer software with which a user can interact realistically using a helmet with a screen inside, gloves fitted with sensors, etc.

5. 'Black' as used here and capitalised denotes a political identity; I use the term in a way which highlights my experience.

6. A rigorous mathematical study of knots.

7. *Dummy,* a dyke magazine, a kind of fantasy hybrid of Quim and Square peg open to everyone who wants to join in. dummy@red-moon. demon.co.uk

8. *Conceptual Physics,* Paul G Hewitt, Harper Collins, 1993.

REFERENCES

Writing For Your Life: A Guide and Companion to the Inner Worlds by Deena Metzger, HarperCollins, 1992.

Writing from the Heart. Inspiration and Exercises for Women Who want to Write by Lesléa Newman, Crossing Press, 1993.

How to Write While You Sleep and other surprising ways to increase your creativity by Elizabeth Irvin Ross, Celestial Arts, 1993.

Narratology - Introduction to the Theory of Narrative by Mieke Bal, University of Toronto Press, Canada, 1997.

Three Steps on the Ladder of Writing, Hélène Cixous, Columbia University Press, New York, 1993.

To Grandmother's House I Go

Jewelle Gomez

SUMMARY. Within the mode of "biomythography" that owes its identification as a genre to Audre Lorde's *ZAMI,* Jewelle Gomez examines her own writing processes. Her explorations revolve around her work-in-process about her great grandmother's life. Issues of truth, memory, history, race, and community are considered. The author also discusses the embodied nature of writing. *[Article copies available for a fee from The Haworth Document Delivery Service: 1-800-342-9678. E-mail address: <getinfo@haworthpressinc.com> Website: <http://www.HaworthPress.com>]*

KEYWORDS. Lesbians, self-writing, body, language, racism, myth, history

---

Jewelle Gomez is the author of five books, including *Don't Explain* (Firebrand, 1998), *Oral Tradition: Selected Poems Old & New* (Firebrand, 1995), *Forty-Three Septembers: Essays* (Firebrand, 1993), *The Gilda Stories* (Firebrand, 1991, which was the winner of two Lambda Awards, for fiction and for science fiction), and *Flamingoes & Bears: Poems* (1986). *The Gilda Stories* was adapted for Urban Bush Women as a play–*Bones and Ash: A Gilda Story,* and it toured U.S. theatres in 1996-97. She has contributed to many anthologies, such as *Best Lesbian Erotica* (1997), and *butch/femme: Inside Lesbian Gender,* edited by Sally Munt (Cassell, 1998). Gomez is the co-editor of *Swords of the Rainbow* (Alyson, 1996), an anthology of gay and lesbian fantasy and science fiction short stories. She was on the founding board of GLAAD (Gay and Lesbian Alliance Against Defamation) and on the original staff of "Say Brother" (WGBH-TV), one of the oldest weekly black television shows in the U.S. Gomez is the former artistic director of the Poetry Center and American Poetry Archives at San Francisco State University and is currently researching her biomythography of her great grandmother.

[Haworth co-indexing entry note]: "To Grandmother's House I Go." Gomez, Jewelle. Co-published simultaneously in *Journal of Lesbian Studies* (Harrington Park Press, an imprint of The Haworth Press, Inc.) Vol. 4, No. 4, 2000, pp. 71-77; and: *Lesbian Self-Writing: The Embodiment of Experience* (ed: Lynda Hall) Harrington Park Press, an imprint of The Haworth Press, Inc., 2000, pp. 71-77. Single or multiple copies of this article are available for a fee from The Haworth Document Delivery Service [1-800-342-9678, 9:00 a.m. - 5:00 p.m. (EST). E-mail address: getinfo@haworthpressinc. com].

Jewelle Gomez
Photo by D. Sabin. Used by permission.

ZAMI, written by Audre Lorde in 1983, is by turns a formal, impos-
ing, conversational and mythic book. It seems to grab daily life as it
drifts down from a fire escape and casts it back up into the sky as both
a drive-in movie and a cautionary tale. Subtitled "A New Spelling of
My Name" *ZAMI* was described by Audre as a "biomythography," a
word she coined to encompass the complexity of her intentions. It is to
this fluid and evocative word that I turn as I examine the life of my
great grandmother, Grace, and try to find the way to tell her story. In
telling of her life I begin, of course, the story of my own.

In an interview in the mid 1980s (*Black Women Writers at Work*, ed.
Claudia Tate) Audre said that biomythography "has the elements of
biography and history of myth. In other words, it's fiction built from
many sources. This is one way of expanding our vision." Audre's
intent, structure and tone in *ZAMI* create a sense of immediacy. This
also helps define biomythography for me, making it ring inside like
the bells of a buoy pointing my way through pea-soup fog into a solid
berth. Her book called to mind the Greek myths, folk and fairy tales of

my childhood. Vulnerable gods, magical animals and ingenious princesses each possessed human and larger than life preoccupations. Elements of truth, wound inextricably around the fantastic, were woven through countless tales over the centuries, reinforcing familiar pictures for each successive generation. There is a ceaseless fascination with the mythic: Edith Hamilton who explicated Greek myths in the 1940s; Wade Davis who tried to penetrate the secrets of Haitian vodoun in the 1980s; Italo Calvino, whose interpretation of Italian folk tales in the 1950s was finally translated into English in the 1980s, or more popularly the contemporary mythology of Xena, Warrior Princess.

ZAMI, however, imagines our lives, not those of gods, priestesses or animals, as both magic and epic, expanding the reader's vision of the past, present and the future. That expansion lies at the heart of all of my writing; finding a focus to help accomplish that has been challenging both emotionally and intellectually.

In my novel, *The Gilda Stories,* and some of my short fiction, I've employed elements of history and myth to relate the stories of the ordinary lives of women, illuminating the extraordinary affects such lives have on others and on our world. Yet those elements are not always so easily accessible. Yes, we can all research things on the net, obtaining obscure, disembodied facts. But what is the psychic, emotional context we use to process the information? None of us is a blank slate (Who'd want to read one?). We each carry inside us the prohibitions and strictures we've bumped up against over the years. Learning to recognize them and "work" them is a process that changes not only what I write, but also how I write. As I did research for *The Gilda Stories,* for example, I started to recognize elements in the mythology that touched me initially because of my Catholic upbringing. Despite eschewing those beliefs in the distant past, the pathways cut by those teachings still ran deep. The textures of ritual, vibrant color, sensory/spiritual connections are characteristics of Catholic and vampire mythology. But examining vampires within a lesbian/feminist context led me in a completely new direction.

If I did research, unearthing figures of the past, historical situations, family dis/connections and did not learn and change it would mean my world is flat, without depth or perspective.

One way I know I'm on the right track with my research and writing is that I sometimes feel, when I encounter a new fact, confused and sweaty. The door I've opened has neither the lady nor the tiger but some completely unrecognizable animal that I'd better get familiar with quickly. With my novel I slipped surreptitiously into the popular mythology of vampirism, twisting and inverting its traditional precepts so that my perspective as a lesbian feminist (rather than the traditional colonialist/patriarchal underpinnings of most vampire fiction) became the philosophical mooring for my set of vampires. But in order to insert myself I needed to first identify with the vampire figure, a surprisingly easy leap.

What resonated for me first was the sense of history such a character would hold. Having grown up with a great grandmother who was born into the Ioway tribe in Oskaloosa, Iowa and who lived to watch the landing of the first astronaut on the moon on television, I'd lived with the expanse of history every day. Other familiar elements were: the sense of being an outsider, existing in opposition to the dominant culture and the isolation that imposed; a longing for forbidden companionship; and resistance to Christian dogma. Being able to make that identification with an "alien" character made my own personal sense of "otherness" (as a lesbian, woman of color, and raised poor) seem almost pedestrian. Creating the idea of a mythic context, the story of my life and that of my characters were then cast against a larger tapestry and implied a sense of the past and the future with which I wanted to work.

Once reinvented, the vampire genre seemed the perfect medium to explore the ideas which sit at my core: examining the connection between power and responsibility, learning how we create "family," making a place in history and speaking to future generations. All of these issues had landed in my lap when I was a teenager in a tenement in Boston's South End and the blood of civil rights activists splashed through my television screen and splattered my existence. Their blood ignited my own, which was already restless with the overwrought gothic of Catholicism.

With the 1960s movement for human rights, the patterns of history became palpable. Artists of the period such as James Baldwin, Sonia Sanchez, Lorraine Hansberry and Audre Lorde all made that history and its relationship to politics intrinsic to their work and their lives. Their typewriter keys were protest signs waved in the belligerent faces of small town sheriffs and big city school boards.

The ensuing years and subsequent movements annealed the concepts of creativity/activism/life for me in ways that no deliberate political indoctrination could ever have done. Participating personally as well as consciously witnessing specific acts that changed generations of behaviour from the past and will affect generations to come is not like watching them on television or reading a history book. It was the lived personal and public experience of phenomenal social change in the 1960s and 70s that made me able to really see myself and set my words vibrating, off the page as well as on. Watching the pages of history turn also helped make all events ripe for mythological treatment.

Thirty years later, as a visiting lecturer in a seminar at The Ohio State University, I looked out at the 15 or so faces of a class in lesbian feminist theory. I answered questions eagerly, but was absorbed by the realization that this particular class had read *The Gilda Stories*–a black, lesbian vampire novel–as one of their texts. The ideas that had forged my life and which had been imbedded in mythic concoctions–earth-laden cloaks, faces untouched by time–had revealed themselves to the professor and to these young students. They perceived, within a genre narrative, my core ideas: we are responsible for our actions today and tomorrow. We make change by how we live. Despite the academic setting they marveled at a popular fiction that confirmed these political ideas.

That this particular readership was focused on lesbians and lesbian feminism seemed particularly appropriate. Although much of the impulse for my writing was formulated during the Black movement, it was the development of a social circle as a lesbian which ultimately coalesced my hunger for the words so they began to form stories. The sense of myself being creative during the Civil Rights era of the 1960s was "other-directed" even as it addressed my issues as a person of color. The oblique omission of a conscious and independent female perspective marginalized women of color and focused our gaze on male standards and goals. Lesbian cultural life of the 1970s and 80s contextualized my female sexual desire as nothing else had.

Audre Lorde wrote in her essay, *Uses of the Erotic*: "The erotic is a measure between the beginnings of our sense of self and the chaos of our strongest feelings." Experience as an open lesbian enabled me to see the political as well as personal ramifications of female and lesbian desire, and begin to perceive the complexities of identity which were merely hinted at by my great grandmother's origins and her sparse memories of them.

When my best friend from high school read *The Gilda Stories*, she too perceived similar messages about responsibility and family. She responded differently, of course; no jargon, but she got the issues and ideas without feeling flattened by heavy rhetoric or abstractions. The appreciation of a Black, heterosexual friend was another bonus I never counted on.

I knew further satisfaction when I was able to adapt this mythology to the stage. Audiences across the U.S. were drawn to the mythic characters despite their "alien" nature. A cross-section of theatre-goers nodded their heads and applauded as if they'd always gone to see black lesbian vampire stories on stage. They, too, were able to make the leap to identify with the core emotional and political ideas the characters raised.

The road to my audience was not very direct. It wound through many dark forests and unpaved patches. There was about a ten year period when I couldn't imagine what I'd write about. The years of illiteracy and silence forced on people of color, jammed down the throats of women, slapped across the mouths of lesbians, built into the paths of the poor, all snapped at my heels, even when I was expanding and solidifying my identity. I'd grown up understanding the power of the media to inform and help reverse public opinion. The narrow, pixillated images of television and movies dominating popular culture in the 1970s supplied neither texture nor context for the work I wanted to do. While I wouldn't have concurred with the dismissal of television or U.S. culture as a "vast wasteland," it was certainly a vast straight white land. I began to question what fiction I could create that represented me, if I didn't always want to write a political essay.

Ironically, it was developing my consciousness as a lesbian of color–pushing me to the furthest margins of the political movements of my youth (which were each implicitly heterosexual), along with my affinity for stories embodying "otherness" in the extreme that enabled me to imagine my fiction within the legacy of U.S. storytelling. The less I tried to fit into the traditional picture (White, American, heterosexual, realism), the easier it was to see myself and write the words that would take their place in our culture.

Now I open my eyes each day with a story in my body trying to find its way out, onto a page and into the world. I have no dearth of stories to tell; the past is now an engine inside me churning out ideas, plots, and characters, blown up to mythic proportions. My only fear is that I won't live long enough to get many of them out. It could take several lifetimes.

After writing for 20 years I still marvel at the decades of activism it took to get me here. Yet I now comprehend the simplicity with which each issue, each identity, was viewed in those tumultuous and exhilarating times. As I look back to the places where my stories began, the unseen facets begin to reveal themselves. I see myself seated on the floor in my great grandmother Grace's house as she combed my hair. I can feel the careful tugs as she tried to tame the cottony mass and hear her low even voice. She's cautious as she recounts the little she remembers of her childhood in Iowa, a mythological place from my child's perspective. Her memories of "Indianness" sit uncomfortably in the air of our Boston tenement, the life of the Black movement swirling around us, dominating the atmosphere.

I wrote that moment down one day because I missed her and wanted to try to remember everything about it. In capturing the rhythm of her combing and talking I discovered a way to reconcile the many elements of her life so the value of her time on earth might be seen and felt.

With the small strands of her memory, Grace had imparted to me a direct refutation of all the information that was conveyed to me through public school education, television, films and books. The demons that John Wayne heroically slaughtered could not be (for me) faceless "bad guys" shrinking at the sound of the approaching cavalry. They were relatives. Just as the movement for human rights in the 1960s made African American history and culture more defined for me and my generation, my research into the Ioway history of Grace (and her Wampanoag husband) further re-frames my sense of self. Searching for those missing parts helps explain who she was. The ordinariness of her life, as when she combed my hair, is what made life extraordinary for me. Her easy enjoyment of modern conveniences such as television, frozen foods and VW vans brought together the past and the present simply, miraculously.

As I dig amongst the shards of history, mythology, and biographical facts my heart pounds with anticipation. No essay can contain the pulsing life implied at every discovery. I might convey the *facts* credibly but, more importantly, I want the reader to feel the tug of Grace's comb and the tentative pressure of her hand. I go to (great) grandmother's house, expecting to find almost anything behind the door, including a wolf. Whatever the facts, fiction, like mythology, is just another way of imagining the truth.

Karla Jay:
An Interview with Lynda Hall

Karla Jay

SUMMARY. Karla Jay discusses *Tales of the Lavender Menace: A Memoir of Liberation* (published in 1999). She engages the connections between the personal and the political in her memoir. The reception by readers, family relations, the history of the feminist movement, racism, and homophobia are also deliberated in relation to the writing "process" and the motivations to write. *[Article copies available for a fee from The Haworth Document Delivery Service: 1-800-342-9678. E-mail address: <getinfo@haworthpressinc.com> Website: <http://www.HaworthPress.com>]*

KEYWORDS. Lesbians, memoir, reader responses, mental illness, sixties radicalism, family

[Editor's note: The following interview was conducted in July, 1999.]

LH: Could you describe the genesis of *Tales of the Lavender Menace*? After so many years of editing anthologies that include autobiographi-

---

Karla Jay is Professor of English and Director of Women's and Gender Studies at Pace University in New York City. She has written, edited, and translated ten books, the most recent of which is *Tales of the Lavender Menace: A Memoir of Liberation.* Her anthology *Dyke Life* won the 1996 Lambda Literary Award in the category of Lesbian Studies. She is editor of NYU Press's series, "The Cutting Edge: Lesbian Life and Literature." She has written for many publications, including *Ms. Magazine, The New York Times Book Review, The Village Voice, Lambda Book Report,* and *The Harvard Gay and Lesbian Review.*

Address correspondence to: Karla Jay, Women's and Gender Studies Program, Pace University, One Pace Plaza, New York, NY 10038 USA.

[Haworth co-indexing entry note]: "Karla Jay: An Interview with Lynda Hall." Jay, Karla. Co-published simultaneously in *Journal of Lesbian Studies* (Harrington Park Press, an imprint of The Haworth Press, Inc.) Vol. 4, No. 4, 2000, pp. 79-86; and: *Lesbian Self-Writing: The Embodiment of Experience* (ed: Lynda Hall) Harrington Park Press, an imprint of The Haworth Press, Inc., 2000, pp. 79-86. Single or multiple copies of this article are available for a fee from The Haworth Document Delivery Service [1-800-342-9678, 9:00 a.m.–5:00 p.m. (EST). E-mail address: getinfo@haworthpressinc.com].

79

Karla Jay
Photo by Jill Posener. Used by permission.

cal writings by gays and lesbians, and providing such a crucial source of understanding and community, the switch to directly addressing your own life experiences is a major one. Was the endeavour always on your mind, or did your particular location in present time and space prompt your writing?

KJ: The genesis for my books comes primarily from the readers and audiences I come into contact with. As I tour with each book, I begin to get a sense of what people want to know more about. In 1992, I began to lecture about the early days of the post-Stonewall uprisings in conjunction with the release of the twentieth anniversary edition of *Out of the Closets: Voices of Gay Liberation* (*OTC*). I was rather shocked by the myths that people believed about the early movement. Generally, young audience members in particular were of the opinion that lesbians were all political but didn't have any sex while gay men weren't political but were continually partying until AIDS came along and the lesbians taught the gay men how to organize political demonstrations and the gay men taught the lesbians how to have fun. The short answer was to scream "NO!," but the longer answer in some ways was to write *Tales of the Lavender Menace*.

Except for some short, humorous essays that involved very specific incidents in my life that were used to demonstrate some larger point, I was reluctant to write about my life. Part of this was a remnant from the early movement. As the co-editor of one of the very first lesbian and gay anthologies (*OTC*), I quickly became a very recognizable figure in the small New York City political community in which I circulated. One day, I left Womanbooks (our local feminist bookstore) with another writer, and the next day word was out all over town that we were lovers, even though we weren't. As a result, I realized that if I were going to survive in the movement, I needed to protect my private life. Having a relationship–or back then, relationships!–was very important to me, and I was often involved with other women whose privacy needed to be respected.

The other major factor was that one of the ways I survived a dysfunctional family was to put the past aside and think about it as little as possible. My mother was mentally ill, and my father's response to that was to keep her at home. People of my generation didn't speak of mental illness–it was a dark secret we kept even from close friends and relatives. I learned at an early age not to bring strangers into the house, and writing a memoir seemed like doing just that. At a young age, I became a sort of parent to my mother, and after she passed away in 1984, I had to take care of my father, who was then in his eighties.

Although my parents caused me a great deal of sorrow–neither one accepted my homosexuality, and my father even denied that I was his child–they were also somewhat childlike and helpless, and I felt responsible for their well-being. Though my parents read very little by the 1980s, I had an aunt we called "the barracuda," who read everything down to the obituaries every day so that she could gloat over the misfortune of others (and verify for herself that she was still alive). She resented the success of her many nephews and nieces, and she went out of her way to spoil whatever luck, whether large or small, might befall others. In 1976, as I recount in my memoir, she outed me to my mother by calling her up at 1:00 a.m. to tell her that I was on the *Tom Snyder Show* and that I was "queer." Then she wrote a letter to my brother, just in case he didn't know about my sexual identity. My mother wound up back in an institution. So I feared that the contents of a memoir would get back to my parents and hurt them.

I had also not said much about my family at work, though my colleagues knew that I flew to Florida to visit them. Having a strange family certainly didn't seem as if it was going to help my tenure bid and promotion–after all, my colleagues were adapting to my open lesbianism. But now, after twenty-five years at Pace, I know my colleagues there like and admire me for who I am and won't confuse me with my family. The people who despise my sexual choices aren't likely to read my books.

LH: This collection engages lesbian self-writing partly from a perspective that the "process" the artist undergoes is a "healing" one. That is a point of view expressed by each of the "subject artists" in my dissertation, and I feel that it is an important one. I suggest that autobiographical writing allows the individual to re-visit/re-create/re-cuperate the past and re-dress past experiences of pain and trauma through their present "act" of writing. Taking control and agency through the present "act" of writing and public appearances, the writer gains voice and creates a "reality" that others may have denied. Did you experience your writing "process" as an ameliorative one? If not, would you say that the more painful family experiences, for instance, had been dealt with already in the past, and that the current writing was a "record" of events, with the significant possibilities of providing witness and survival strategies for others? For instance, you write, "Perhaps my account will comfort those who also suffered in silence for fear of damaging the image of the movement. Perhaps it will give them permission to speak of their pain without fear of condemnation" (*Tales* 265). Did the writing "process" bring YOU comfort?

KJ: The writing process did not bring me comfort. Indeed, there was a great deal of pain in revisiting my family in such an intimate way. There were times when I wept as I wrote and envied my brother, who has coped with our childhood by amnesia. Since I don't believe in psychoanalysis, revisiting old wounds only opens them once again. I also don't harbor romantic notions about "healing." The last time I saw my mother she was sitting in a hospital room trying to change the TV channel with an electronic device that moves the hospital bed up and down. She thought it was a remote. She weighed 85 lbs., most of her ribs were broken from osteoporosis, and she had terminal cancer in her lungs and brain, which they had just discovered. She was only 72 years old. She didn't recognize me at first and asked me how I knew which room she was in. When she figured out who I was, she turned back to the television and ignored me. Though the doctors thought she might live up to eighteen months, I was certain it was the last time I would ever see her alive. There was no Hollywood scene of reconciliation, and she died two days later.

Though I hadn't intended to write about my family when I started the memoir, I realized that readers wouldn't be able to understand the process of political analysis unless I brought my family into it, because it was through consciousness raising, rather than through analysis, that I learned to understand my mother and how she had been pathologized by society and by my father.

Another element that I did come to understand, not through the memoir, but through a disastrous relationship with a former partner, was that my family had left me totally unequipped to recognize aberrant behavior in others. I used that understanding of my life to reflect in the memoir about how many radicals refused to deal with anti-social and fringe behavior in others–for example, Shulamith Firestone's failed attempt to shove a magazine editor out a window.

Another painful issue to revisit was the incident in which some teenagers, in a failed robbery attempt, threw me down a flight of steps and fractured my spine in three places. I had once written about the attack as a meditation on the limits of pacifism. The assault, which paralyzed my right leg for a couple of months, convinced me that women need to learn self-defense. I hadn't thought about my back for a long time, in part because it had stopped bothering me many years ago, but during the process of writing the book, my right hip and right leg started to hurt again. At first, I thought it was just a pain memory, or too much sitting due to the tight schedule my publisher insisted on, so I ignored it until I couldn't sleep because of the pain. Finally, I had it looked at and, writing had injured my back.

LH: "Coming out" is a never-ending process, and you discuss the implications in your "Epilogue." Could you briefly discuss in more detail the major role that "writing" has played in the "coming-out" process for you, and then, in terms of other lesbians' autobiographical writing? It is no surprise that in the letters I am receiving from many of the individuals who are contributing to this project they mention pain at the "silences" and "hiding" they enacted in relations with their families over the years, and then, in addition, possibly the close family members die without ever having really "known" them as they are. "Writing" is one way to "come out" to those who mean the most to us?

KJ: Within the LGBT community, we tend to think of "coming out" only in terms of revealing sexuality, but many of us have other secrets–dysfunctional families (and families are dysfunctional by nature), alcoholism, drugs, sexual abuse, s/m fantasies or behavior–things we assume others can't deal with. We tend to endure in silence, but blame, guilt, or the complexities of survivorship can mar our lives if we're not careful. Luckily, wonderful writers like Dorothy Allison have addressed incest and Pat Califia and others have spoken out on alternative sexualities, but there is little written on some issues. Each of us who speaks out about difference makes others stronger.

LH: In the *New York Times* book review (April 4, 1999), Stacey D'Erasmo describes your memoir as a "bittersweet meditation on the mutability of self." In my introduction, I suggest that the writing process often brings a sense "wholeness" and constitutes a gathering together of fragments and gaps of past life experiences. I sense a different dynamic in your statements regarding your writing, with "distance" from the past selves an element, rather than a gathering together, or putting the pieces together and embracing them in the present. You state, "I often felt I was writing about someone else, some long-dead, distant relative whose name escapes me. I am no longer the person at the center of this political autobiography, not even vaguely. Though I sometimes laughed or cried as I recalled poignant memories, I felt little connection with the person I was writing about" (*Tales* 263-4). Could you address the "self" in terms of these dynamics?

KJ: Stacy D'Erasmo was very astute in describing my book as being a "bittersweet meditation on the mutability of self." For some, writing the memoir may bring a recognition that we have always been ourselves, smaller versions snuggled within us like Russian dolls. But for me, I have changed dramatically over the years and probably will do so again. There are some things that seem constant over the years–my sense of humor, my loyalty to friends, my passion for justice. But I've survived for thirty years in the movement because I could change, because I realized that the movement would never support me and that

I would have to find a career to do so. Luckily, I became a professor, which I love. I take great joy in my students. But I'm also ready to move on to other selves and look forward to retirement as a path to exploring new ideas and hobbies.

One interesting development was that when I wrote the memoir I felt very alienated from the radical I was writing about, but as I began to speak about those times in bookstores and on radio programs around the country, I got much more in touch with my passion for social justice, which has expressed itself in tamer ways over the last twenty years or so. I started to identify more with the radical positions I thought I had left behind. Part of it is that the climate in this country is becoming increasingly conservative, and the lynching of black people and queers has outraged me. But each fresh killing brings a burst of anger, after which people return to their quotidian behavior because there's no broad-based radical movement anymore to sustain ongoing demonstrations in our communities.

LH: In your emails I sense an absolute sense of joy at the tremendous positive response you are receiving from readers. As a reader, there are no adequate words to describe my admiration and appreciation for your openness and candid writing about your experiences, and the delight at your writing style and the aesthetic quality of the book. I don't know what I expected, but it is hard to have anticipated such a rich combination of the personal and the political. Could you discuss your reaction to the enormous positive response the memoirs are receiving? In particular, since you are doing so many "readings" to promote the book, could you talk about the "immediate" response at readings, both in the sense of your feelings about having written the book, and in terms of facilitating community in such an immediate and effective way?

KJ: In writing a memoir rather than a social history, I was honoring the radical tradition of writing about oneself rather than presuming that I could speak for/as others. However, the most common reaction I get from people over the age of forty is that they're deeply grateful that someone has written about *their* experience. As Linnea Due wrote in *Bay Area Reporter*: "No longer must I struggle to explain what it was like in the late '60s and early '70s; I need only hand over Jay's book. . . ."

The radical sixties may be in vogue right now, but the contributions of feminists and the lesbian, gay, bisexual, and transgendered communities have been erased in popular portrayals of that era. Movies like the television film *The Sixties* downplayed the struggle of black people for civil rights, and the rest of us apparently didn't exist at all! The men were the activists, and the women slept with them, but that scenario ended for many of us by 1968 and never existed for others. I think there is a real sense in which feminist history and lesbian history have been erased, and there's a joy in seeing even the small correction a memoir like mine can offer. Too many of the achievements of the Women's Liberation Movement have been completely forgotten–boiled down by the media to one misrepresented action at the Miss America pageant in 1968 where bras were never burned. The many other wonderful actions–our sit-ins, takeovers, and organizing efforts have been forgotten.

Some of the people who showed up at bookstores, having already read the book, also were concerned that our achievements were being erased or that their own accomplishments were disappearing from historical accounts. This is a very real problem, more so for feminists than for queers, because few archives are collecting feminist material. But many books have to be written before the full scope of people's contributions is understood. Because a cast of thousands would be impossible for readers to follow, I consciously reduced the number of people as much as possible. I focused on some fresh figures who hadn't appeared in other accounts; but still, that appears to erase the others. There's no easy answer to this problem, except that many more voices need to be heard.

Another thing that people responded to is the fact that I was bi-coastal, and I recognize the large contribution that activists outside New York made to the movement. Far too much history has been New York-centric as well, erasing the gains fought for by women all over the country–all over the world.

LH: Are you planning to write additional memoirs?

KJ: Now that I've done some self-writing and the sky didn't fall in, I have other times in my life I'd like to write about, such as spending part of grade school in a "slow learners'" class or being swept off my feet by a countess when I was living in Paris in the 1970s. But I have other plans to pursue first and am currently at work on a murder mystery.

Memories in Flesh and Marble

Anna Livia

SUMMARY. This piece is about writing and having children and the places they occupy in my life. It describes a sense of isolation, of being cut off from others like me and my efforts to recreate connections, in fiction and in flesh. I explain how I came to be the mother of twins and recount some of the battles fought with doctors, midwives and strangers, as well as between my lover and myself. Lesbian motherhood may no longer be an oxymoron, but it is an awkward, uneasy category open to endless, hostile questioning from outsiders. Better to write our own stories, around lived contradictions, than accept our inscription under erasure on doctors' forms and birth certificates. *[Article copies available for a fee from The Haworth Document Delivery Service: 1-800-342-9678. E-mail address: <getinfo@haworthpressinc.com> Website: <http://www.HaworthPress.com>]*

KEYWORDS. Lesbians, self-writing, lesbian motherhood, medical establishment, twins, birth

I first dreamed about having children in India. I had visited the Taj Mahal. "A memory in marble," isn't that what the *Baedeker Guide*

Anna Livia has a PhD in French Linguistics from U.C. Berkeley. She is currently a Visiting Professor at Berkeley. Livia is the author of five novels, including *Bruised Fruit*, published by Firebrand (1999), and two collections of short stories. *Pronoun Envy*, a revision of her dissertation, is forthcoming from Oxford University Press in their new series on Language and Gender. With Kira Hall, she edited *Queerly Phrased*, published by Oxford University Press, the first comprehensive collection of articles on language, gender and sexuality. She is currently working on a book on gay use of computer-mediated communication entitled *Hexadecimal Homos*.

Address correspondence to: Anna Livia, PhD, French Department, Dwinelle Hall, U.C. Berkeley, Berkeley, CA 94720 USA (e-mail: livia@cal.berkeley.edu).

[Haworth co-indexing entry note]: "Memories in Flesh and Marble." Livia, Anna. Co-published simultaneously in *Journal of Lesbian Studies* (Harrington Park Press, an imprint of The Haworth Press, Inc.) Vol. 4, No. 4, 2000, pp. 87-96; and: *Lesbian Self-Writing: The Embodiment of Experience* (ed: Lynda Hall) Harrington Park Press, an imprint of The Haworth Press, Inc., 2000, pp. 87-96. Single or multiple copies of this article are available for a fee from The Haworth Document Delivery Service [1-800-342-9678, 9:00 a.m. - 5:00 p.m. (EST). E-mail address: getinfo@haworthpressinc. com].

Anna Livia
Photo by Linda Brocato. Used by permission.

calls it? I gazed at the gleaming white mausoleum, at the two towers placed either side, leaning slightly outward, away from each other to give the impression of parallel lines. Given the usual rules of perspective, a sharp ninety-degree angle would have forced the eye to interpret the towers as leaning inward. I listened to the story of the Moghul king who had erected this architectural splendor to house the mortal remains of his beloved wife, Mumtaz. Then I looked again at the long path that leads toward the Taj, the sleekly groomed gardens to either side, and I saw the people who were not there, the people shut outside the gates, the poor of India. I felt tricked, lulled into tranquillity by the beauty and peace of this place. The walls of the Red Fort keep out the modern India, in favor of this memory in marble, which even on the hottest day remains cool, silent, somehow stagnant. The Taj guide continued with a tale of the King's long days spent gazing out the window of the Red Fort at the palace he had built around the body of his queen. Must beauty always be created on the bones of the dead? Can great love have no other expression than the changeless face of eternity?

That night I dreamed of people locked out. I am in one room of a palace, my lover is in another. The two rooms drift apart like rafts on an ocean. The ocean is full of bobbing rafts. The rafts of friends, family, and ex-lovers are being swept further and further from mine. I feel my lover and me separating. I feel the distance of my family in Australia, of nieces and nephews growing up to whom "Aunty Anna" is no more than a yellowing photograph pinned to the fridge door under a Mad Max magnet. I feel the separation from friends I know in London. There are many rafts headed in different directions, pulled by currents and cross-currents. Then I turn my attention to my own raft. I have just given birth to a tiny baby girl named Asha, Hindi for hope.

I am not insensitive to the loneliness, anguish and despair of the Moghul king grieving for his lost wife. I know the Taj Mahal was a work of hope, an artistic creation that would live on, another hundred, thousand lives in the eyes of those who look upon it. I have tried to replace my own lost loves in worlds I create. My mother and adored baby sister left me when I was sixteen. My father died when I was twenty-five. I have spent years bringing them back in stories and novels. I have strived to remain in contact with lovers and friends left on other continents, but the litany of names gets longer and longer as I grow older, and many are names from languages no one around me speaks any more: Mwela and Komalo in Central Africa; Nônô and Llonka in Mozambique; Amarnath and Aneil, Indian brothers from South Africa; Fernando who was murdered when Samora Machel's plane was shot down over the Drakensberg.

But, like the towers of the Taj Mahal, in order to preserve the illusion of parallels, I distort the story itself. Julius, who dies in Rwanda in my current manuscript, is not the Mozambiquan Fernando, but both are confirmed Marxists whose mothers were Catholic; each wonders if he will go to the same paradise as his mother when he dies. Closer to home, the kind, compassionate Beryl of *Minimax* and *Relatively Norma* is more like the mother I would have liked than the woman who abandoned me in my adolescence. Out of bitterness, rage and loneliness, I rewrote us both, the daughter understanding, forgiving, generous, the mother receptive, approachable, optimistic.

Sometimes, the real story is so hidden only I can retrace its outline. I once had a lover who was very ill. She got sicker each day until she seemed about to die. She asked me to promise to kill her if she grew too weak to do it herself. Horrified, I refused. She was angry. I gave up arguing, feeling only increasing horror, and no compromise in sight. Instead, I wrote a story called "Pamelump" about an eleven year old white girl in Africa whose best friend was born without arms or legs. This friend asks the girl to help her commit suicide because she does not want to grow up dependent on others. In it I rechanneled the anger and despair I felt about my lover's repeated requests and refusal to take "no" for an answer.

Many of my friends in London are writers, and I greet their new books eagerly, seeing traces of them in novels about Jewish devils or Polish refugees. Patricia Duncker's *Hallucinating Foucault,* Caro Clarke's *The Wolf Ticket,* Ellen Galford's *The Dyke and Dybbuk,* Suniti Namjoshi's *St Suniti and the Dragon,* bring me memories carved in marble and transformed into art, with all its shifts and glides, its deceptive planes and rough edges. As writers, we live on in our stories, and our stories change our memories of the past.

Hearing that I was born in Ireland, grew up in Central Africa, went to high school in London, that my mother and sister emigrated to Western Australia, that I spent two years in France, my lover Jeannie asked, "Where is your home, Anna?"

I picked my books off the shelf, ten at the last count, five novels, two collections of short stories, two translations from French, and one academic anthology, and laid them down on the bed where she sat. "Here, Jeannie. This is my home." Even as I said it, it sounded cold, silent, stagnant. It was not enough. She wanted children, she said, and to stay in Berkeley forever and grow old and die there. This was the first time it had occurred to me you could make a choice to stay in one place simply because you liked it there. You could beach the raft, build a family on dry land.

I had not forgotten my dream in New Delhi, about the baby named Asha, Hindi for hope. But life went relentlessly on, with its cracks and fissures, its separations and anguish. My family had always moved, looking for work, fleeing from unnamed terrors no less felt for being unspoken. I was hired as assistant professor at the University of Illinois and it did not occur to me to turn the offer down, any more than it occurred to me at that point that "family" could be something I made, rather than something I endured. The following summer I drove back to Berkeley to rent a room in Jeannie's house during the three-month vacation.

As soon as she saw my car pull up, Jeannie jumped up and ran out the front door to meet me. "I'm ovulating!" she said exultantly, "Tomorrow I'm going to the Pacific Reproduction Center to be inseminated. I want you to come with me."

I had been driving for three days solo, across two thousand miles of cornfields, plains, and mountains. I looked fondly at the slight figure with the mass of black hair and smiled, bewildered but cheerful. "Okay," I said. This simple, unconsidered affirmative was to change my life.

Next day, I watched while Jeannie pulled off her jeans and underwear and jumped joyfully into the stirrups. I hadn't seen her naked since we broke up four years before, so the sight of her sitting on the edge of the bed with her legs spread was somewhat jarring. From that moment, events moved forward inexorably. Two weeks later, Jeannie learned she was pregnant. Three weeks later, she and I became lovers again.

Compared with my more tempestuous relationships, this one started very simply. Jeannie invited me for a walk in Tilden State Park to look for owls one evening. I gazed up into the eucalyptus trees, looking for owls while she gently told me she had brought me there under false pretences. She still felt as though we were lovers, did I feel the same. I did. I asked rather solemnly if it would be okay if I kissed her. It was.

We never really discussed what a baby would mean to our relationship. Jeannie had been trying to get pregnant for more than a year. There was no question for her but to continue on the path on which she had embarked. For me, since Jeannie was pregnant when we got involved for the second time, it felt like being with her meant agreeing to raise a child. Eleven weeks after the insemination, Jeannie had a miscarriage. No baby. But those weeks of expecting a child had changed me. Now I wanted one; I wasn't simply bowing to an inevitable biological process.

At the end of the summer, I had to drive back to Illinois for one more year as a professor. It occurred to me that this might be the last time I taught a class, and the thought made me very sad. I liked my students; I liked my colleagues; I liked the university and I was a good teacher. My last class was on francophone African film, a course I had devised as a way to create a community for myself of people who had seen the same vibrant, hard to get hold of films I had. I wanted someone to talk to about the incredible visions of directors like Djibril Diop Mambety and Souleymane Cisse. It was, of course, also a way for me to regain some link to my African childhood.

By April, Jeannie was pregnant again, and I had given notice at Illinois. This time we were expecting twins. I told no one, fearing another miscarriage. Jeannie and I held excited discussions about names, wanting to have several ready for the different possibilities twins offer. "Emma Livia" and "Naomi Julian" if they turned out to be two girls. "Livia" and "Julian" are both given names of mine. "Asher Julian" and "Emil Elijah" if we had two boys. "Emma Livia" and "Asher Julian" if it was a boy and a girl. Somehow the name "Asha," or "Asher," had become terribly significant since my dream in India.

Twin pregnancies are hard. Jeannie weighed only one hundred and eight pounds before she got pregnant and she put on weight much slower than the doctors wanted. There were endless "invitations to worry," as Jeannie put it. She wanted a homebirth, and it took some time for us to find a midwife willing to deliver twins at home. She went on seeing an HMO doctor for routine blood work, lab tests, ultrasounds and fetal monitoring, but this doctor was dead set against home delivery.

At first, I didn't have much of an opinion either way. The war between the homebirth midwives and the hospital doctors felt like a round of the banshees versus the military, with me and Jeannie stuck in the middle of the combat zone. It was Jeannie's body and therefore her decision as to what happened to it. Gradually, however, the sound of the two tiny heartbeats on the doppler, the sight of the foetuses yawning and putting their thumbs in their mouths on the ultrasound, made the presence of the babies real to me. There were two other people whose lives depended on our decisions. From an observer in the wings of a fascinating biological process, I became involved in a more immediate, visceral way. I became aware not only of how Jeannie was treated, but of how I was treated and how we were treated as a lesbian couple about to have children.

Since Jeannie was so clear about her own vision of how her pregnancy and delivery were to go, since she opposed every non-essential test, every potential risk to the foetuses, she was not well liked by the HMO doctors into whose carefully regulated world she refused to fit. Not only was she a difficult patient, she was an articulate, intelligent, highly educated, upper middle class difficult patient. While Jeannie refused to fit into the one size fits all category of institutionalized pregnancy, there was no category for me. The first time I met the HMO doctor, she said "And you're Jeannie's mother?" looking a little doubtful since I'm only six years older than Jeannie. "No," I said, surprised, "I'm her partner." There was no space for "partner" on the form, so she put me down as the babies' father.

"How old are you?" she asked, and duly wrote down my answer in the "father's medical history" slot. "How much do you weigh? What is your general health like? Any family history of mental illness?"

As I sat answering these ridiculous questions, I remembered the previous year when Jeannie had come in for an ultrasound at eight weeks only to discover there was a "problem." She had been whisked away to another radiology department where the lack of fetal growth was confirmed and she was offered a D and C. I had sat on the end of the bed, unable to see the ultrasound screen, unable to hear the doctor's voice. No one told me Jeannie was by then carrying a dead baby. I resented having to guess.

Now, a year later, we had fine, healthy babies and we wanted to keep them that way. So, of course, did the HMO and the midwife. I wanted to feel included in the process, but this was a much more controversial desire. The HMO did not recognize my existence and the midwife never spoke to me directly unless Jeannie was out of the room. I imagined this latter behavior was due to some feminist belief in the primacy of the pregnant woman, but it made me feel excluded nonetheless and hurt so much that it in the end I gave up attending her weekly visits. I began to feel much more sympathetic to fathers.

As the pregnancy progressed, tensions between me and Jeannie grew. By eight months, it seemed that one twin, Baby A, was nearly a pound heavier than the other, Baby B. The doctors wanted to induce Jeannie and put both babies in the NICU. Jeannie was adamantly opposed, demanding a second ultrasound–which did not confirm the discrepancy in weights–and insisting that she carry the babies to term. She believed their best chance for growth and health was to remain inside her as long as possible. I found the resulting tensions unbearable, especially since I had no control over the outcome. I was intensely worried about Baby B, and I agreed with the doctors that his best chance was to be born prematurely and supported by machine, even though his sister did not need this.

I say "he" and "his sister" because by now we knew the sexes of the babies. Baby A was a girl, Emma Livia, lying head down against Jeannie's cervix; Baby B was a boy, Asher Julian, lying transverse across Jeannie's upper abdomen. They were real to me. I had been talking to them for months inside Jeannie's belly. The last thing I wanted was a fight with Jeannie about them that I knew I could not win. It was the wrong time to discover we had very different attitudes toward the medical establishment. Jeannie, daughter of a nurse and a psychology professor, saw doctors as her equals, possessed an impressive amount of medical knowledge herself, and had always got prompt medical treatment for any illnesses or accidents she had had. I, daughter of a secretary and an impoverished writer, had often been left without medical care because my family was too poor to pay for it. Attending a series of open clinics in London as a teenager I had been brutalized and sexually abused by a number of doctors. These experiences left me with a mixture of hatred and terror of the medical community, accompanied by a paradoxical yearning for all the goodies western medicine could provide.

Friends, this part of the story ends happily, if you can call birth an ending. The twins were born vaginally at Alta Bates hospital, induced on Pitocin a week after the due date because Jeannie had been unable to go into labor spontaneously. Emma was vacuumed out at 8:40 a.m., weighing 5 pounds 10 ounces. As soon as Emma was born, the doctor put her hand through Jeannie's cervix, grabbed hold of Asher's legs and pulled him out at 8:43 a.m., weighing 4 pounds 15 ounces. Both babies were healthy, and we all went home twenty-four hours later. As I drove back to our house, I was filled with an extraordinary sense of responsibility and joy. My whole family was in the car and I was driving. I was no longer on a raft out at sea alone, watching my loved ones bobbing around on waves which were taking them further and further away from me. We were going home.

That part of the story, the most important part, is mostly a happy one. The children are now four and a half months old. I love them so much it takes my breath away. The first three months were, from my point of view, absolutely ghastly. Not only were we living on practically no sleep, but there never seemed to be a moment when our arms were not full of one baby or the other. I was worried about finding work, having been without a job for six months. Jeannie and I had not been able to talk easily about the tensions that started during her pregnancy and our relationship was so new I lacked the comfort of remembering times when we were more united. Somehow things changed. The babies began to sleep on a more regular schedule. I got employed to teach two courses at UC Berkeley–one of them on francophone African film. It was not tenure track, but at least there would be some money coming in. Jeannie and I had a fight, survived weeks of hostility and cold silence, to emerge sweeter and kinder at the other end. The other night we even managed to get the babies to sleep early enough, and for long enough, so that we could sneak into the bed in my room and make love. For lesbians, sex and motherhood do not go together easily.

The part of the story that remains ragged and unhappy is the tale of my desire for inclusion and the endless bars put between me on one side, and Jeannie and the babies on the other. Small instances, small slights, stupid ill-considered remarks that add up. When Jeannie was six months pregnant, we joined a group called Twins by the Bay. A local TV company contacted the group wanting to do a piece on bringing up twins. For us, this meant getting up at 5:30 in the morning in order to be at the house of another twin mom so the show could air at seven. The presenter proceeded to interview each little family unit in turn, with lots of cute shots of twin babies and anodyne questions about teething, feeds and sleep patterns. When he reached Jeannie, however, he made sure the camera rested on her, cutting me off at the shoulder so that only my left arm was visible. He asked her about the pregnancy, as though she were the only one involved. It turned out that our midwife's girlfriend worked for the same TV station and could get us a copy of the tape.

"You should put the tape with the babies' album," the midwife suggested enthusiastically, "Their prenatal TV appearance."

"Put it with the rest of memorabilia that excludes me," I snapped, "The baby books where you cross out 'father's name' and write in 'co-mother,' the birth certificates that list you as mother, leave the father blank and have no place for me."

After the babies arrived, I became even less visible. The night after they were born, I slept at Jeannie's side in a metal hospital cot. At 3 a.m. two nurses came in to check on Jeannie and the babies. Emma cried at being woken up. "Shh," said the nurse, "You'll wake your grandma." Since I was clearly not a man and therefore not the babies' father, but yet was sleeping beside Jeannie, I must be the children's grandmother. In the morning, another nurse came in and saw me holding Asher while Jeannie was in the bathroom. "Are you the grandmother?" she asked.

Two weeks after the birth, Jeannie got the symptoms of what seemed to be flu, but might have been a uterine infection. The four of us bundled up and went into the hospital. While Jeannie was being examined, I sat outside with the babies, picking them up, rocking them, singing to them, making growly animal noises for them. It was a Sunday and there was only a skeleton staff on duty so we were there almost two hours. I fell into conversation with one of the other women waiting who asked friendly questions about the babies' weight, names, sexes and sleeping patterns. Finally Jeannie was through and rejoined me to start the journey home. As she came toward us, the woman I had been talking to looked at her and said,

"She sure has her hands full, hasn't she?"

I stared at the woman, feeling as though I had been slapped in the face. "Do you think my hands are empty?" I asked as I carried the babies toward the door.

But these outside events, enraging and painful though they may be, are less important than the daily process of getting to know the babies. Noticing that Asher likes animal sounds, I made up a story full of moos and growls and barks. It is about a little boy who goes for a walk in the forest and encounters all sorts of animals who frighten him with their noises so that he runs away, hides, climbs a tree, swims a lake, and finally ends up back home where his mother points out that the animals just want to play with him. It ends with the line, "And so Asher learned not to be afraid, and not to make a fuss." I typed it up and put it in his baby book as my contribution. Emma used to love lying on her tummy and being swung around like an aeroplane. I made up a song for her about 'Emma the Aeroplane.' It rejoices in lines like "She's dropping in on Heaven in a 747 / Yes she's going in a Boeing 'cos she likes the to-and-froing." This too is in the baby book. More original and more personal than "father's occupation" or "paternal grandfather's first name."

So my children have become part of my life; they are both characters in my stories and the audience for other stories. They anchor me to the present and provide links to the past. But they are memories of flesh as well as marble. Berkeley is a long way from New Delhi, but the towers which frame the Taj Mahal have remained my most vivid memory of India. In order to look like parallels, they lean apart, united by the beautiful mausoleum.

Writing My-Self-Body

Mary Meigs

SUMMARY. The author traces her changes in attitude toward her body, sexuality, and public disclosure of her lesbianism through reflections upon her writings as the years pass. She addresses the connections between the body and writing, and celebrates the community of lesbian writers who push outward the boundaries of language to assert that there are no boundaries. *[Article copies available for a fee from The Haworth Document Delivery Service: 1-800-342-9678. E-mail address: <getinfo@haworthpressinc. com> Website: <http://www.HaworthPress.com>]*

KEYWORDS. Lesbians, self-writing, body, memory, aging, publishing

When, in 1978, I started writing my first book, it was to be my coming-out as a lesbian but I didn't think of myself as a lesbian writer.

Mary Meigs was born in Philadelphia in 1917, and grew up in Washington, D.C. She graduated from Bryn Mawr College in 1939, studied painting after World War II and had one-woman shows in Boston, New York, Cape Cod, and Paris. She moved to Quebec in 1975. Her first book, *Lily Briscoe: A Self-Portrait,* published in 1981, was followed by *The Medusa Head* (1983), *The Box Closet* (1987), and *The Time Being* (1996), all published by Talonbooks, Vancouver. She performed with six other women over sixty-five in a Canadian National Film Board semidocumentary (1988)–*The Company of Strangers.* She wrote about the saga of being in the film in a volume entitled *In the Company of Strangers* (Talonbooks, 1991); this book won the Quebec Society for the Promotion of English Language and Literature Award for Non-Fiction in 1992. She is currently mulling over a book about losing a twin sister, old age and dying.

Address correspondence to: Mary Meigs, 427 Grosvenor Ave., Westmount, Quebec, Canada H3X 2S5.

[Haworth co-indexing entry note]: "Writing My-Self-Body." Meigs, Mary. Co-published simultaneously in *Journal of Lesbian Studies* (Harrington Park Press, an imprint of The Haworth Press, Inc.) Vol. 4, No. 4, 2000, pp. 97-100; and: *Lesbian Self-Writing: The Embodiment of Experience* (ed: Lynda Hall) Harrington Park Press, an imprint of The Haworth Press, Inc., 2000, pp. 97-100. Single or multiple copies of this article are available for a fee from The Haworth Document Delivery Service [1-800-342-9678, 9:00 a.m. - 5:00 p.m. (EST). E-mail address: getinfo@haworthpressinc.com].

Mary Meigs
Photo by Rollie McKenna. Used by permission.

Like many other lesbians of that time I believed that one could be a writer pure and simple, a genderless writer, and I was suspicious for the wrong reasons of Freud's insistence on sex as the driving force of human life. I was under the illusion that my writing was the voice, not of my body, but of my mind. "In my family," I wrote, "the body was unmentionable and sex was a secret subject along with its precise vocabulary, and innocent words that might suggest it." I felt proud of having shed this attitude, and yet the word *lesbian* terrified me and I was unable to say it out loud, certainly not about myself, though for some reason this was easier in writing than in speech. In retrospect I understand that I wrote the book in order to *make* myself come out, to stop pretending and to name myself without shame. But though I had fallen in love with and lived with women happily for more than thirty years, even though as narrator in *Lily Briscoe: A Self-Portrait* I write about the ecstasy of prolonged kisses (no physical details, however) with another woman, it is noteworthy that in both of the sex-scenes with a man I close my eyes to hide the alarming sight of his love-making.

In *The Medusa Head,* I talk about falling in love as though it were a kind of blitzkrieg: "It invades one's entire being, either as a blessing or a sickness . . . one is bewitched and invaded against one's will." The one love scene in *The Medusa Head* is distinguished by failure and frustration. "Her sign was Aries and the paradox of Aries was contained in the hard head and the softly insistent tongue that failed to melt my petrified sensuality. . . . I recognized in myself a lifelong need to punish any desire or indeed any exercise of will that demands too much of me . . . For instinct had always told me that sexual possession gives absolute power, the power to say, 'you are mine!' To be Andrée's was to be in mortal danger, to lose not only my body but my soul." I had not yet realized that the body is one of the soul's voices. The mind's words, too, are part of the body's speech; they can assume the airborne form of happiness or the heavy weight of grief, depression or anger.

While I was writing *The Time Being* I felt for the first time that a lesbian body guided my words which begin with a direct translation of my imagined love-state into words of sensual joy. They sang a virtual love scene which was repeated when it became real. As I wrote about the identity of imagined and real, reliving it simultaneously, the cells of my body seemed to voice themselves as words without the loss in translation that words often suffer. It must be every writer's dream to find words as immediate as musical notes. It was mine as a lesbian writer to find an instrument to play this story of two old women in love. My light-filled memories gave me airborne words that echoed the imagined. In telling about love's failure too, I tried to recapture memories of how it felt–the strange dead weight of it. "Marj, weighted by the heaviness of old age, feels heavy and awkward. She is fighting with the sickness in her heart, her stony unforgiving. Her time being with Kate has become time choked with dust, with monstrous trivialities." Her body seems to be one with the landscape: "She is looking at a landscape emptied of birdsong; the clearcut mountainside, the silence reflects her own breakdown of memory." In each of my books my happiness or my heaviness of being have seemed to be echoed in the moods of the landscape around me.

It was my dream to make this story of two old women in love as musically audible to a reader as it was to me. I used the words and cadences that I've always used, borrowed from a lifetime of reading mostly men's books along with great women novelists and poets, among them Virginia Woolf and H.D., who were among the few who blazed a new experimental trail in language. In the last twenty years lesbian-feminist writers have brought about, through their own work, a metamorphosis of language. I think with admiration of Betsy Warland, Daphne Marlatt, Gail Scott and Quebec writers Nicole Brossard, Marie-Claire Blais, Louky Bersianik and Jovette Marchessault, how each of them has made a new language from her own vision and has pushed outward the boundaries of language to assert that there are no boundaries. It has the mysterious power "to say what I didn't know I meant" (Warland); "to read one's body, that vast text (60,000 miles of veins and arteries)" (Marlatt); to live in her poetry a "concentration of the *power* of language, which is the power of our ultimate relationship to everything in the universe" (Adrienne Rich). Susanne de Lobinière-Harwood, who set herself the subtle task of translating Nicole Brossard's work from French to English, saw it as a challenge "because it demands that kind of intimacy of thought, that kind of idea-transfusion in the branching veins of language."

The language of lesbian writing has changed the voice of lesbian eroticism, a song of physical immediacy and oneness which lesbians have always sung.

Even if I now speak this language with the accent of old age, old habits and an undependable memory, every coming-out since the first one in 1981 has meant a step forward toward an integration of the community in myself, toward listening to the endless conversation between genes, cells, particles of DNA in my single body that contains identities with all the living organisms on earth. Not literal listening, of course, but a kind of awareness of how and why we are who we are. The progressive comings-out in my books have given me the courage to write an erotic scene in the most recent one, erotic for me, at least, which is one more step toward freeing me from the cautious person who wrote *Lily Briscoe.* I had been writing self-censored lesbian books all along but now have a surer understanding of what freedom can mean in the writing of the next one.

A.D., A Memoir:
Excerpts

Kate Millett

SUMMARY. These excerpts are reprinted from Kate Millett's *A.D., A Memoir,* a book in which Millett reflects upon her early life and her life-long deep love for her Aunt Dorothy. Aunt Dorothy was the benefactor who financed Millett's Oxford education; she died in 1984 without ever accepting Millett's choice of lifestyle. As well as deliberating the devastating effects of homophobia, Millett contemplates several of her books and discusses the writing process, the circumstances surrounding the writing, and the reception of her books by her Aunt Dorothy.

KEYWORDS. Lesbian, body, self-writing, publishing, family, homophobia, politics

. . . She makes friendly ironic reference to the footnotes in *Sexual Politics,* but the rest are anathema. I had sent her *The Basement* that

Kate Millett is a major, internationally acclaimed feminist thinker and writer. She has published extensively, including *A.D., A Memoir* (Norton, 1995), *The Politics of Cruelty* (Norton, 1994), *The Loony-Bin Trip* (Simon and Schuster, 1990), *Going to Iran* (Coward, McCann, 1981), *Elegy for Sita* (Targ, 1979), *The Basement* (Simon and Schuster, 1979), *Sita* (Farrar, 1976), *Flying* (Knopf, 1974; Ballantine, 1974), *The Prostitution Papers* (Ballantine, 1973), and *Sexual Politics* (Doubleday, 1969).

These excerpts reprinted by permission of the author, Kate Millett, and by permission of W.W. Norton & Company.

Address correspondence to: Kate Millett, THE FARM–An Art Colony for Women, 20 Overlook Rd., Poughkeepsie, NY 12603 USA.

[Haworth co-indexing entry note]: "A.D., A Memoir: Excerpts." Millett, Kate. Co-published simultaneously in *Journal of Lesbian Studies* (Harrington Park Press, an imprint of The Haworth Press, Inc.) Vol. 4, No. 4, 2000, pp. 101-106; and: *Lesbian Self-Writing: The Embodiment of Experience* (ed: Lynda Hall) Harrington Park Press, an imprint of The Haworth Press, Inc., 2000, pp. 101-106.

summer but she found the book incredible. Life on another planet, too terrible. We had been trading puns on the nature of tragedy over the telephone when I called to ask permission to visit and tabled the discussion only to forget it when together. So *The Basement* failed. But before I left I tried to foist my books on her with a bovine love-sickness. If only to validate, give proof, that whatever I did or was said to me–I had done this. I had not made children, nephews or nieces, not made money or a good marriage, but I had these real and tangible proofs of my existence; I had produced these objects and these alone. You could hold all I had done in fifteen years under one arm, or both arms, counting the mass of *Going to Iran* which I had the temerity to present as well, mere typescript, still not even in print. But together with Mother she was referred to in the text and she should know beforehand, if only to object before publication. She wouldn't bother. She wouldn't even bother to accept it in its black spring binder. No, absolutely not. Then the *Elegy for Sita*; this is a rare edition. There were only three hundred fifty copies printed; each is signed. Isn't it lovely paper, the edges haven't even been cut. "No, I detested *Sita* and I do not want this either." "Really–" stung past tears, the sheer sur-prise of it, this slap. I clutch at the notion that perhaps it is jealousy of Sita, as I have told myself for years that perhaps it was jealousy that made her so angry to start with, over Jaycee, that I had gone to Oxford with "another woman." When she should be my all–this invented romance of mine. (162-163)

*   *   *

[Editor's note: The second excerpt begins with reflections on the impact that a magazine article about Millett's life had on her family relationships. The thoughts are addressed to her now deceased Aunt Dorothy, and Millett includes deliberations on *Sexual Politics*.]

Of course you dealt with the press all your life through the society columns which are rather kinder than the treatment meted out to radi-cals and women's libbers disturbing the peace, so you could be airy about newspapers and claim it never mattered what they said as long as they spelled the name right. With the two t's. As a feminist I expected every improbable lie; as a radical I even understood their reasoning in the lies they chose. But it simply did not occur to me that the members of my family would be grist for anybody's mill. Or that my father would read a magazine some kindly or unkindly neighbor made sure reached his bedside following a serious heart attack and just upon returning from the Mayo clinic, and die a few days later, perhaps also in grief at what he had read about himself.

Only months after he and I were reconciled. For we had been friends again after twenty-one years of silence and estrangement. Which Mother imposed but his sisters transcended, sending him east by airplane to see me and Mallory, knowing he was old and ill and near dying. Fumio knew it too and saw it in his eyes: "He is already a ghost but very beautiful." How good this reunion. May, the May before *Sexual Politics* was published in July. The newspapers, the television, the late summer and the fall. And then the attacks. In November, *Time* says I'm queer and therefore my book is suspect, its footnotes might even be inaccurate, my learning and my argument are fallacious because I have "confessed," "admitted" to being a homo-sexual. Actually I was busy flaunting it and gay liberation, but now am said to confess and admit and am canceled. *Time* had me on the cover in August but being ill my father missed it; being at the Mayo until Christmas he hadn't picked up on old publicity–a proud man, his daughter's book gave him great delight. She had done something; she is in the papers. *Time* had this version of my life: "A father who beat her and her sisters, then walked out on them when she was 14" (*Time* August 30, 1970, 18). An unsigned article "researched" by a reporter who haunted me for days, riding along in the next seat in airplanes, angling for missteps, statements out of context. They had boiled our existence to a tabloid brutality. My father is handed this absurd ugly false public identity just as he is about to die. He was home again with his second wife and children at Christmas but his voice was faint and hard to hear. A neighbor had loaned him all the magazines. "You must be careful how you read that stuff, Dad; they have all sorts of axes to grind when they write about us." "Sure, honey." Another week and he was gone. And now I stand here in A.D.'s house on the lake and she tells me some lousy magazine article helped push him over the edge. No, damn it, no. I will not buy that nor be party to it either. I do not write that junk; it is written about me and I have no control whatsoever, cannot even sue since they are way too damn smart to get nailed at anything, have boxes full of lawyers to get them off the hook; it's a business–you don't "say," you "imply"; you say a person is "said to" be this or that, etc., rather than "is." "Listen, I loved my father; I would never have put those poison-pen sons of bitches on him; I hate what they say; it hurts me too. I have hated this; I have hated the whole damn thing."

In my entire life I have never raised my voice before her. She grows quiet and listens. Something of understanding forms in her eyes of what it has been, who I am. She almost trusts me; I am almost one of them. A warrior too, but one on the scrappy side at the front: real blood, not inherited money; public trouble, not divorces or quiet private bankruptcy. But finally I'm improbable.

Mother and sister Sally know something of where I stood: they know politics, they know feminism, they know the chances, the hopes for success, the dangers, the public infamy of lesbianism; they also shy away on behalf of the married lady in the suburbs who obsesses Sally, or the dilemma of the verdict of respectability versus humanity's final claim for its rights which worries Mother. Yet both would protect me and see me through despite disagreements in tactic, even in principle.

But with Dorothy there is only the tribe. The Milletts. Family. Their name and fame and fair honor. *Sexual Politics* was a treatise to be proven like a well-made tract; she once teased me that the footnotes were reliable because she had gone to the trouble to check them periodically through the book. I can see her chuckling her way through her library. "You win on your footnotes; you persuade by the weight of your references." As if it were merely a big crossword puzzle. My father was beautifully, movingly persuaded by what I said. My aunt being a woman of course knew all this stuff already and even having it said did not impress her; what interested and amused her was the manner of saying these things. But she could not admire entirely; she really had to tease erudition and pedantry.

In the first glow of its aftermath, before it became a newspaper nightmare, I could still crow over it to my aunt. Probably a little less pompous than when I came home chock-full of Brit scholarship from Oxford; thirty-five now, a bit less obvious, comical. "You see, I was trying for a combination of English critical writing–you know, relaxed, civilized, not your hard grinding American treatise on the number of commas in a Richardson novel–and then throw in a bit of direct American plain talk too. Outside the academy but not quite the Bowery," I said to her. Proud of myself and newly published, made much of: one leg crossed, a hand hugging my ankle, wearing slacks for the visit, fancying myself before her as I probably never had on any previous occasion. "Hmmm," she said, trying not to smile, smiling anyway. (224-228)

* * *

[Editor's note: In this excerpt Millett recollects her preparations for writing *The Politics of Cruelty*.]

So of course this morning I am alive fairly early, unable to sleep, curious to discover if I actually have a headache. Not really. Because today is my fifty-first birthday and I am as earnest about it as a child. With a Virgo's list of what to achieve in the coming year. Yesterday I ticked off what I'd done since fifty, then reduced it all to finishing a book, which seemed a sufficient if lonely task. But next year, the research against torture, the next book. You must also draw every day. And plan sculptures for a show the following year–last night Erna actually recalled the cage sculptures I made ten years ago. Flattery and gratitude astonished me. So that's on the list even if prematurely. Underline that you've got to draw every single day. Use the darkroom too. Further down the list are grander, increasingly crazy schemes: renovate the blue barn next summer, re-side it, save the beams, sheathe them again safe–forever–it will be perfect, rain-tight. Further flights into tractor repair, the fantasy purchase of a brand new, actually virgin, machine, not our usual twenty-year-old cripples. Narrow, lithe, pretty new paint, a slender wheelbase so as not to kill trees. On and on in this vein. Then the Bowery: move the kitchen, install another Franklin stove–after all, this is just a list–cross out one stove and put down two. Never mind getting the six hundred pounds up the stairs, the expense, the nuisance plumbing the gas pipes.

Make everything snug so you can study all day, never leave the place, steep yourself in the literature of political prisoners, the corruption of South American dictatorships, the collusion and manipulation of North American government and business. You have four years ahead of you to absorb and reflect the sufferings of interrogation, state terrorization, the locked door, the cell. I want to do a sculpture of a group of people sitting calmly on folding chairs inside a cage, I told Erna last night. And outside the cage are another group sitting calmly on folding chairs watching them, facing them. She put her arm around me and we laughed out loud. That said it.

But saying it in print is different, longer, harder: the profusion of details, factual and emotional, symbolic and actual, metaphorical and metaphysical. Quixotic stab: to try just by writing about it, thinking about it, feeling it, to make others feel it, care, get mad, be ashamed, make waves, refuse to put up with it–torture. Climbing the funny ladder Richard has made out of two-by-fours which brings one, however perilously, up to the loft bed while balancing the second cup of coffee, I realize I'm scared to death of this job ahead of me, find it hard to discuss with myself even in private, avoid thinking about it sometimes. Of course it's a big intimidating project–but until this moment I did not realize just how frightened I was. Having realized that, perhaps now I can start; knowing I'm scared is always my beginning. (312-314)

Shani Mootoo:
An Interview with Lynda Hall

Shani Mootoo

SUMMARY. Shani Mootoo discusses her creative process, with a particular focus on her novel *Cereus Blooms at Night.* She elaborates on the writing process in relation to other forms of art, and explores the relationship of her characters in *Cereus Blooms* to her own life experiences. *[Article copies available for a fee from The Haworth Document Delivery Service: 1-800-342-9678. E-mail address: <getinfo@haworthpressinc.com> Website: <http://www.HaworthPress.com>]*

KEYWORDS. Lesbians, self-writing, body, child sexual abuse, racism, colonialism, cross-gender identification

LH: Many of the writers who are participating in this collection on lesbian self-writing processes are also visual artists, such as Mary

---

Shani Mootoo is a writer and a multimedia visual artist. Her novel *Cereus Blooms at Night* (Press Gang, 1996; McClelland and Stewart, 1998) was shortlisted for the Giller Prize in 1997 and was long-shortlisted for the Booker Prize. She has published a book of short stories, *Out on Main Street & Other Short Stories* (Press Gang, 1993). Her writings have appeared in various anthologies. She produced and performed in the video *Wild Woman in the Woods* (1993), collaborated with Wendy Oberlander on *Paddle and a Compass,* and created and performed in *Her Sweetness Lingers.* Mootoo had an exhibition at the Vancouver Contemporary Art Gallery–*Shani Mootoo: Photocopies and Videotapes, May 28 to July 9, 1994.*
Address correspondence to: Shani Mootoo, #223 2556 East Hastings Street, Vancouver, B.C. Canada V5K 1Z2.

[Haworth co-indexing entry note]: "Shani Mootoo: An Interview with Lynda Hall." Mootoo, Shani. Co-published simultaneously in *Journal of Lesbian Studies* (Harrington Park Press, an imprint of The Haworth Press, Inc.) Vol. 4, No. 4, 2000, pp. 107-113; and: *Lesbian Self-Writing: The Embodiment of Experience* (ed: Lynda Hall) Harrington Park Press, an imprint of The Haworth Press, Inc., 2000, pp. 107-113. Single or multiple copies of this article are available for a fee from The Haworth Document Delivery Service [1-800-342-9678, 9:00 a.m. - 5:00 p.m. (EST). E-mail address: getinfo@haworthpressinc.com].

Shani Mootoo
Photo by Kathy High. Used by permission.

Meigs, Maya Chowdhry, Mary Wings, and Kate Millett. Could you describe the relationship of your writing "process" to your creative "process" in painting, photography, and video production? Would you say that the writing is a more satisfying and "telling" way of expressing your "self"? Is this a progression? Do you feel that writing is the creative mode that might solely occupy your time now and in the near future?

SM: Man loves man, man loves woman, woman loves woman. That was the last line of one of the first pieces of what might be called creative writing I ever did. I was about ten years old then. The poem was entirely idealistic, full of rainbows, golden sunsets, deer (which in Trinidad I had never seen, except in images of more northern climes) and perfect love, where gender was no obstacle to coupling. Just like a true artist, every scribble I did, I had to run and show it off; but this last line caused much consternation and dread in the adults in my environment. Questions as to my meaning followed, and a lesson on society's mores followed.

Even before that incident I had tried to tell my grandmother that one of my grandfather's friends was touching me in ways and in places that felt uncomfortable. Poor woman, fearing the wrath of my grandfather, and perhaps of her daughter who had entrusted her with my care, and certainly scandal, she told me never to say such words again.

I was getting a clear message again and again. I remember clearly thinking when I was about ten years old that words, which I believe were my first love, were getting me in trouble. I remember thinking that I needed some way to be able to express and flush out the complicated ideas and feelings I had as a child, and then I was trying to figure out how I could continue to do this without the public use of words. While I continued to write, but in obscure sentences and phrases that only I could decipher (poetry!), I started to concentrate more on picture making which I felt had more potential than words for ambiguity and equivocalness.

It was not until years later, when I was in my late twenties, that I was forced to come face to face with the demons of child sexual abuse. It was then that I actually began to use those dreaded words to speak out what had happened, only to find that in more sympathetic situations, those same words were being heard, encouraged, and believed. Validation was almost intoxicating, and I found myself driven to find the most correct words, phrases, sentences, analogies, and stories to unequivocally tell and explain to myself and to others what had happened to me, how I felt, and why I have become the person I am.

The early discouragement never interfered with my love for words. That remained intact. But the discouragement turned out to be something of a gift: I learned to express myself, to flee, to find and invent myself and my world in another medium, pictures and images. I work in three media now, two-dimensional visual art, video, and various forms of writing. I use pictures and video, and to some extent poetry, to dis- or re-order my world, while I use word-based storytelling to try to "speak out" my life, but not just to tell what has/had happened to me. Also to try to break down the world, even the pain and trauma of the world into smaller parts, that are step-by-step logical, so that I, and others, might understand, and rage against or sympathize with it.

There is, for me, less of a need to flush out or to try to explain its ecstasy, but a desire to express it abundantly.

I like being able to work in different media. Abstract ideas, images, stories are my first impetus. Sometimes I receive ideas with a medium already prescribed by the idea; sometimes it is even a complete idea whose execution is "all" that is needed. Sometimes I must make a decision as to which medium is best suited to the idea. If I start with a desire to use a specific medium first, and then must fuss around to find an idea, I am certain of failure. The content of the work, nine and nine-tenths of the times, comes first.

LH: Many writers describe the characters in their books as representing different parts of themselves–either of their present sense of self or of parts of selves of the past that have long been left behind. For instance, in her piece for this collection, Jewelle Gomez suggests that there are parts of her "self" in different characters in *The Gilda Stories.* In *Cereus Blooms at Night,* the wide array of characters cross many boundaries–racial, gender, sexual, class, and age. Would you say that to some extent you are writing your "selves" into being? And, if so, in what ways? Andre Lorde refers to the "telling" of experience, and part of Lorde's meaning in that phrase is the "telling" or the "relating" of parts of oneself in order to share the experiences. In your experiences with your readers and their responses, do you find that there is a readerly desire to locate a "reality" in some of the stories told?

SM: The first delight in writing, for me, is the invention of stories, situations, events, where I can impose my own vision of how things would be in my ideal world. My ideal world is not void of the lower states of existence, that is, of anger, hellishness, hatred, greed, etcetera. But in my ideal world these states are out-smarted, or given the slip by good, truth, beauty and innocence. Writing itself is a way of giving the slip to the traumatic aspects of my own life-experience. It is a way of re-ordering a world in which many aspects of my own self have been denied or injured. This re-ordering, in my made-up worlds of fiction, does not attempt to pulverize "bad," but is a way of "permission." Permission to exist as a woman, a woman of color, as a lesbian, within–not on the out-side of–the everyday world of society.

The stories I write are not agenda-driven, but I have found that I am most passionate about a story line when it is an appeal to the larger world for acceptance for me and for people like myself–as we are, not as the larger world would like us to be. Tyler, the main narrator in *Cereus*, I have come to realize, does just this. But so do other characters who resemble me less than Tyler does. For instance, Hector, the straight gardener, tells Tyler of his little brother Randolph who as a little boy was taken away by their mother and placed in a mission home so that their father wouldn't be able to beat him anymore for his girlish ways. Not only did Randolph suffer, but through this separation and ostracism, so did Mr. Hector and their mother. This situation is for me an appeal, as it were, to my own family perhaps, for acceptance and inclusion, and is a way of showing up the ridiculousness of discrimination. Mala, the main character in *Cereus*, is not, as everyone in the novel thinks, a madwoman, but she is someone who has found extraordinary ways to survive incest and abuse and society's neglect and scorn. Mala gives up verbal language, while I use verbal language to detail her trauma and her triumph. To my mind, her abandonment of this language and my use of it are only different sides of the very same coin.

In the novel that I am working on now the main character is a straight, older man who is in love with a straight older woman. When they were children his mother used to be her mother's housemaid. It is a story partially of class struggle. I find that I empathise with this man. In many poignant ways I know his story intimately–if "lesbian" in relation to a straight world, might be viewed as a classed position.

Writing, putting words and grammar and meaning to task, is for me a way to begin to comprehend, and to tell, to expose, to appeal, to re-order and to overcome.

LH: In the introduction to this collection I suggest that self-writing offers the opportunity to ameliorate past (and present) abuse and painful experiences through the individual writing their "reality" into being and assuming the authority to define their own experiences. As well as creating a "reality" for the self through the writing process, the writer also provides witness for others. The readerly witnessing "act" creates community, and understanding through that community; as well, the writings encourage social transformation by actively intervening to disrupt the cycles of abuse. Do these dynamics resonate with your own writing experiences?

SM: I want to emphasise again that when I set out to write a story, its impetus is usually some very compelling image, a picture in my mind, or a phrase that pops into my mind and it is so intriguing, or good-sounding that I am provoked to run after it and see where it wants to go. I do not set out with an agenda, as in "I have something I must say, or explore, regarding childhood sexual abuse. Maybe I will write a story and say my piece/peace." I have tried to do this, especially when given the task of contributing a piece of fiction to a themed collection. I have tried to make artwork, including video, addressing some ideal or ideologue, only to find that the didacticism that invariably results is disruptive to the art aspect of the work.

The idea for *Cereus* began with an image, that picture-in-my-mind, of an old woman with wild, unkempt hair, standing over a pot on a stove, steam billowing into the room as she placed handsful of snail shells into the pot. I wanted to write the image down, but as it was it was nothing more than a description. As I wrote I began to feel the slightest nudge of familiarity with this woman, some unconscious knowing of her, and that was the initial compulsion toward a story: who was she, and why was she doing this bizarre act in her kitchen. I did not intend to fill her life, her story, up with my own personal story. It was long after the book was published, and I began to hear back from readers their take on it, that I realized from what they were telling me that I had drawn on my own experience, in some instances so very closely that I was telling my own story by imbuing Mala's life with mine.

It is true that when I was a child, not yet five years old, I attempted to tell my grandmother about the family friend who was sexually abusing me. She did hush me, and told me, no doubt because of her own panic and inability to deal with it, not to say such a thing again. In some ways the people of the town in my novel might be a mirroring of that experience with my grandmother. But every other memory of that grandmother is delightful, and if I were asked to look back on my life and choose the person in it who was the most compassionate and loving towards me, and with whom I felt safest, I would pick her. Tyler's indulgent and supportive grandmother is very consciously drawn on my own grandmother. But Tyler, to my mind, is also repre-sentative of my grandmother. His "hearing" and support of Mala was surely an unconscious re-working of my grandmother's response to me. Through Tyler's more aggressive self-agency–which does not come easily to him, but is a studied strength for survival–I re-write the consequences of disclosure.

The writing of these characters and their many stories, when I chose to forget the daunting challenge of writing a novel for the first time, was, in another aspect, thrilling. What was so thrilling was drawing out, frame by frame, rather than in a generalised way, why–and that is the most important thing–why–why what happens happens. Anything else is mere description of events. But what excites me is, through storytelling, trying to understand why things happen. Not to explain them–because from my point of view that would be didactic, but rather to figure out why they happened in the first place.

The Truth About Writing/ Writing About the Truth

Lesléa Newman

SUMMARY. The essay examines how one writer turns her life experience into fiction, and explores the question so often asked of fiction writers, "Is that story really true?" Author Lesléa Newman uses her own work to show how the experience of losing her good friend, the poet Gerard Rizza, to AIDS, translated into a short story, a children's book and a novel told in fifty poems. Each form tells a different sort of truth about the experience the author went through in her process of assimilating her grief into her life and her work. *[Article copies available for a fee from The Haworth Document Delivery Service: 1-800-342-9678. E-mail address: <getinfo@haworthpressinc. com> Website: <http://www.HaworthPress.com>]*

KEYWORDS. Self-writing, AIDS, lesbians, gay men, death and dying

I am giving a reading in a bookstore, an auditorium, a café–it doesn't matter. I am reading a poem, a short story, a novel excerpt–

Lesléa Newman is an author and editor whose thirty books include *A Letter to Harvey Milk* and *In Every Laugh a Tear* (fiction); *Still Life with Buddy* and *The Little Butch Book* (poetry); *Writing from the Heart* (nonfiction); *Out of the Closet and Nothing To Wear* (humor); *My Lover is a Woman: Contemporary Lesbian Love Poems* and *The Femme Mystique* (anthologies), and *Heather Has Two Mommies* and *Too Far Away to Touch* (children's books). Her literary awards include fellowships from the Massachusetts Artists Foundation and the National Endowment for the Arts. Her newest book, *Girls Will Be Girls: a novella and short stories,* was published in January 2000.
Poems appearing in this essay are © 1997 Lesléa Newman.
Address correspondence to: Lesléa Newman, P.O. Box 815, Northampton, MA 01061 USA (www.lesleanewman.com).

[Haworth co-indexing entry note]: "The Truth About Writing/Writing About the Truth." Newman, Lesléa. Co-published simultaneously in *Journal of Lesbian Studies* (Harrington Park Press, an imprint of The Haworth Press, Inc.) Vol. 4, No. 4, 2000, pp. 115-124; and: *Lesbian Self-Writing: The Embodiment of Experience* (ed: Lynda Hall) Harrington Park Press, an imprint of The Haworth Press, Inc., 2000, pp. 115-124. Single or multiple copies of this article are available for a fee from The Haworth Document Delivery Service [1-800-342-9678, 9:00 a.m. - 5:00 p.m. (EST). E-mail address: getinfo@haworthpressinc.com].

Lesléa Newman
Photo © by Mary Vazquez. Used by permission.

again, it makes no difference. After I finish reading there is a sweet moment filled with applause. Then I inform the audience I am happy to entertain questions. Immediately a hand shoots up near the back of the room and I know the question I am about to be asked: was the story (poem, novel excerpt) I just read true?

I always hesitate before answering that question, as I try to sort out the feelings I have about it. On the one hand, the question is a compliment to any fiction writer, the implication being: *what you just read was so convincing, it had to have happened in exactly the way you told it.* On the other hand, the question is an insult to any fiction writer, as it implies complete denial of the writer's imaginative and creative powers: *what you just read was so convincing, you couldn't possibly have made it up.*

Sometimes when I'm asked if a story is true, I'll pull a Bill Clinton and reply, "That depends on what you mean by true." Other times I rely upon a stash of quotes I have gathered just for this occasion. Grace Paley has said, "Any story told twice is fiction." Frederic Raphaell declared, "Truth may be stranger than fiction, but fiction is truer." My favorite quote of all states, "I lie in order to tell the truth." (This last quote has been attributed to everyone from Mark Twain to Pablo Picasso. I am not sure who was the first person to say it.)

Once in a while there is a slight variation to the way the question is phrased: "How much of that story is true?" When this happens, I follow the example of an old writing teacher of mine and give a random number. "Twenty-seven percent," I'll say. Usually the asker of the question will nod her head thoughtfully, maybe even jot down my answer, and sit back in her seat, satisfied.

But the truth is–and there's that word again–everything I write is true and none of what I write is true. If I took apart any story or poem I have ever written–even the ones that are based on events that actually happened–and ask myself if the circumstances recounted in the story occurred in the exact way I presented them, the answer would be a resounding *no*. When I write, what I try to do is capture the emotional truth, or heart of the story. As C. Day Lewis said, writers "do not write in order to be understood. We write in order to understand." I write in order to make sense of the world–the world inside me, the world outside me and the relationship between the two. What I write is not *the* truth. It is merely *my* truth.

When I teach writing workshops, I always find it easiest to explain this concept by example. I have two students stand up and have an interaction: a dialogue, a duel, a dance. Then I have all the students in the class, including the two participants, write a description of what just happened. The inconsistencies and contradictions are astonishing. We all witnessed the same event, yet no two descriptions are ever very much alike. Which version is true? One could say none of them. Or one could say all of them.

In my own writing, I find that I tell the same stories over and over again, revealing different layers of the truth like peeling a never-ending onion. Robert Coover has said, "Borges said we go on writing the same story all our lives. The trouble is, it's usually a story that can never be told." One story that has had a tremendous impact on my life and on my writing is the loss of my friend, the poet Gerard Rizza, to AIDS.

The first story I wrote about Gerard is called "With Anthony Gone," and it appears in my book of short stories, *Every Woman's Dream* (New Victoria Publishers, 1994). (As an interesting aside, when I wrote the story, I did not know that Gerard's middle name was Anthony, yet that is the name I chose to give the character based on him.) "With Anthony Gone" takes place at Anthony's memorial. As the protagonist of the story, a young lesbian named Joanne, travels to the community college where Anthony once taught and where the memorial is being held, she reminisces about her friendship with Anthony. How they met in Boulder, Colorado and became roommates. How they studied poetry with Allen Ginsberg together. How Anthony met his lover, Mark, who also became a friend of Joanne's. How a man named Ben rounded out the group into a foursome. How the sexual tension between Ben and Joanne (who was straight at the time) was never resolved.

When Joanne arrives at Anthony's memorial, she feels like a stranger. Though they always stayed in touch, her life and Anthony's went off in different directions, and their contact over the last few years has been sporadic. As she sits there, she hears her name called by Ben, whom she has not seen in many years. They leave the memorial, find an empty classroom, and suddenly find themselves engaged in a passionate kiss. The kiss leads to an embrace, which leads the characters dangerously close to doing something they know they don't really want to do. Both characters are profoundly shaken by this experience; in the end Joanne realizes that finally having a sexual encounter with Ben (something Anthony had always urged her to do) is pointless: it won't bring Anthony back. The story, which is told in Joanne's voice, ends:

> I turned and left the room and the building without looking back. With Anthony gone there was no one I really wanted to talk to. There was no one to share the great irony of the moment with and that was a real pity, let me tell you. With Anthony gone, there was nothing to do but head up the street even though I had absolutely no idea where in the world I was going.

So, how much of the story is true? The facts are these: I did meet my friend Gerard in Boulder, Colorado; we did live together; and we did study poetry with Allen Ginsberg. Gerard did meet his lover Keith while we lived in Boulder, and Keith did become a good friend of mine. And another gentleman, who shall remain nameless, did hang out with us, a gentleman for whom my feelings at that time would best be described as a "crush."

The part of the story that sprang from my imagination, but which I feel captures my emotional truth, is the section that details what happens when Ben shows up at Anthony's memorial. The actual person based on Ben did not attend Gerard's memorial. However, another man whom Gerard and I both knew from our days in Colorado did show up. I sat next to him and cried on his shoulder. When he comforted me with a hug, I felt a closeness with him I had not previously experienced. The hug lasted all of fifteen seconds. Then we parted and I never saw him again.

This experience stayed with me, and my inner fiction writer began asking the all-important question, "What if?" What if a lesbian bumped into a man she had once had a crush on at a friend's funeral? What if the lesbian and the straight man had once had a mutual attraction? What if their shared grief turned into a shared passion? How would they be affected? How would they change? How would they remain the same? These are the questions I attempted to answer as I wrote the story.

The next story I wrote about Gerard was a children's book entitled *Too Far Away to Touch* (Clarion Books, 1995). This book describes a young girl named Zoe and her relationship with her favorite relative, her Uncle Leonard, a gay man living with AIDS. Uncle Leonard takes Zoe to the planetarium, where they see a show about stars. Zoe asks Uncle Leonard, "How far away are the stars?" He replies, "Too far away to touch, but close enough to see." This becomes the refrain of the book, as Uncle Leonard pastes glow-in-the-dark stars on the ceiling of Zoe's bedroom, and then takes her to the beach where she can see the stars, "for real." As they lie on a blanket and look at the stars, Zoe asks her uncle about his health, and where he will go after he dies.

"I don't know where I'll go," Uncle Leonard says, "but I know where I'll be. Too far away to touch, but close enough to see."

At the end of the book, Zoe and Uncle Leonard see a shooting star. Though it flashes across their vision for only an instant, Zoe understands that it isn't really gone, because when she closes her eyes she can still see it in her mind, just as she will always be able to picture Uncle Leonard, even if someday she won't be able to physically see him.

How much of this story is true? I never had a gay uncle living with AIDS who took me to the planetarium and to the beach. Yet truthfully, when my friend Gerard died, I felt helpless as a child. My grief was as bottomless as that of a howling infant railing at the unfairness of life. I wrote *Too Far Away to Touch* to express myself, and to comfort myself. My hope for the book was that it would bring comfort to children (including Gerard's two nephews) who had also experienced such a profound and utter loss.

Still Life with Buddy (Windstorm Creative Ltd., formerly Pride & Imprints, 1997) is a novel told in fifty poems about the passionate friendship between a lesbian and a gay man living with AIDS. Buddy is a composite character, based mostly on Gerard, but with bits of two other friends who died of AIDS thrown in: the writer Stan Leventhal and the scholar Victor D'Lugin. Interestingly enough, though the character, Buddy, is not "real," he became very real to me as I spent months writing about him. It was as though my friends were with me, urging me to write about the truth of their lives so that a small part of them could stay alive and remain vital. The poems that comprise *Still Life with Buddy* came pouring out of me at breakneck speed. Paul Monette, who wrote a brilliant cycle of poems after his lover died that became the book *Love Alone: Eulogies for Rog*, said, "Writing (them) quite literally kept me alive." I believe composing the poems contained in *Still Life with Buddy* was absolutely essential to maintaining my mental health at the time I was reeling from the deaths of my friends.

In addition, my need to remember and honor my friends pushed my writing to a new and exciting level. I had never written fifty poems on a single subject before and my efforts were rewarded by a Poetry Fellowship from the National Endowment for the Arts.

Though I had different experiences with each of my friends as they lived and died, I felt writing a book that focused on one character living with AIDS would make a stronger statement. Each poem in the book has a different ratio of fact/fiction in it. For example, "Once Upon a Time" describes a watch worn by Buddy:

with no hour hand
no minute hand just a second
hand that swept
round and round
his wrist endlessly.

When I said to Buddy,
"What time is it?"
He always answered, "Now."

    In the above poem, Buddy is based on my friend Gerard, who loved
Yoko Ono's art piece "Clock of Eternity." I imagined Buddy wearing
a watch that imitated Ono's statement on time. I did once hear Gerard
answer "Now," to the question "What time is it?" Thus the poem
came together in my mind.
    "Buddy's Pantoum" is based on a day I spent with my friend Stan
in the hospital. I recorded the events of that day as accurately as I
could remember them. The lulling rhythm of the pantoum captures the
dream-like, surreal quality of what was happening at the time:

Buddy's Pantoum

I sit in the hospital with Buddy
He is thin as the IV pole by his bed
Buddy gasps for breath, holding on for dear life
As his roommate's TV bursts into laughter

He is thin as the IV pole by his bed
His skin is so hot it burns my hand
As his roommate's TV bursts into laughter
Buddy's doctor snaps on two rubber gloves

His skin is so hot it burns my hand
His empty eyes are full of fear
Buddy's doctor snaps on two rubber gloves
loudly, like a teenager cracking her gum

His empty eyes are full of fear
He hesitates, then clears his throat
loudly, like a teenager cracking her gum
He says, "Buddy, when your heart stops. . . ."

He hesitates, then clears his throat
Time stands still in the airless room
He says, "Buddy, when your heart stops
should we let you go or bring you back?"

Time stands still in the airless room
Buddy's lips move but he doesn't speak
"Should we let you go or bring you back?"
The only sound in the world: a commercial for Diet Coke

Buddy's lips move but he doesn't speak
"If you don't decide, we're legally obligated to save you."
The only sound in the world: a commercial for Diet Coke
The doctor peels off his gloves, chucks them into the trash

"If you don't decide, we're legally obligated to save you."
Buddy groans, rolls his head on the pillow, side to side
The doctor peels off his gloves, chucks them into the trash
gives a little wave, leaves me and Buddy alone

Buddy groans, rolls his head on the pillow, side to side
His roommate who always hears everything
gives a little wave, leaves me and Buddy alone
I take his hand, ask him what he wants

His roommate who always hears everything
despite his attempts to appear asleep
I take his hand, ask him what he wants
His voice slow and thick, "I don't know how to decide."

Despite his attempts to appear asleep
I know Buddy is trying hard not to cry
His voice slow and thick, "I don't know how to decide.
I can't think about it now. Tell me a story."

I know Buddy is trying hard not to cry
I rack my brain for something to say
"I can't think about it now. Tell me a story."
"Once upon a time, there was a boy named Buddy."

I rack my brain for something to say
I sit in the hospital with Buddy
"Once upon a time, there was a boy named Buddy."
Buddy gasps for breath, holding on for dear life

And then there are poems in the collection that are not factually true
at all, but speak a different kind of truth, nevertheless:

Fun with Buddy's Meds

Pour them
into a jar and shake it
to a Tito Puente tape
Buddy always liked a Latin beat

String them
into necklace & earring sets
and wear them to a drag ball
Buddy did love to accessorize

Feed them
to the rats in the hall
and watch them puke all night
Remember Buddy's sick sense of humor?

Line them
up on a table take
a hammer smash them
one by one by one

The above poem does not describe what I did with my friends' medications after they were dead; it describes what I would liked to have done with them–an accurate, emotional truth.

These days I have a new answer to the question, "Is that story true?" When asked, I smile mysteriously and quote the poet Muriel Rukeyser: "What would happen if one woman told the truth about her life? The world would split open."

Truer words were never spoken.

NOTE

WORKS CITED

"With Anthony Gone," ©1994 Lesléa Newman from *Every Woman's Dream* ©1994
Lesléa Newman (New Victoria Publishers, Norwich, VT).

Too Far Away to Touch ©1995 Lesléa Newman (Clarion Books, New York, NY).

"Once Upon a Time," "Buddy's Pantoum," "Fun with Buddy's Meds" ©1997
Lesléa Newman from *Still Life with Buddy* ©1997 Lesléa Newman (Windstorm
Creative Ltd., formerly Pride & Imprints, Port Orchard, WA).

Striving to Be Selfish

Ruthann Robson

SUMMARY. In "Striving to Be Selfish," Ruthann Robson explores the different kinds of selfishness it takes to be a writer and a dyke, especially the necessary focus on the higher self. Distinguishing the writer from the author (and the dyke from the lesbian), she argues that there is an almost spiritual dimension to the practices of writing and sex. *[Article copies available for a fee from The Haworth Document Delivery Service: 1-800-342-9678. E-mail address: <getinfo@haworthpressinc.com> Website: <http://www.HaworthPress.com>]*

KEYWORDS. Self-writing, selfish, sex, dyke, writer

Being a writer, like being a dyke, is essentially selfish.

It takes a tremendous amount of selfishness to become a writer or a dyke. In both instances, one must put oneself first and foremost. A

Ruthann Robson's latest book is a collection of short fiction entitled *The Struggle for Happiness,* published by St. Martin's Press in 2000. Her previous books include two collections of short fiction, *Eye of a Hurricane* (1989) and *Cecile* (1991), both published by the lesbian/feminist Firebrand Books, and two novels, *Another Mother* (1995) and *a/k/a* (1997), both published by St. Martin's Press. Her volume of poetry, *Masks,* with an introduction by Marge Piercy, was published by Leapfrog Press in 1999, and a new volume of lesbian legal theory, *Sappho Goes to Law School,* was published by Columbia University Press in 1998. She is Professor of Law at the City University of New York School of Law, one of the very few progressive law schools in the world.

Address correspondence to: Ruthann Robson, CUNY School of Law, 65-21 Main Street, Flushing, NY 11367 USA.

[Haworth co-indexing entry note]: "Striving to Be Selfish." Robson, Ruthann. Co-published simultaneously in *Journal of Lesbian Studies* (Harrington Park Press, an imprint of The Haworth Press, Inc.) Vol. 4, No. 4, 2000, pp. 125-130; and: *Lesbian Self-Writing: The Embodiment of Experience* (ed: Lynda Hall) Harrington Park Press, an imprint of The Haworth Press, Inc., 2000, pp. 125-130. Single or multiple copies of this article are available for a fee from The Haworth Document Delivery Service [1-800-342-9678, 9:00 a.m. - 5:00 p.m. (EST). E-mail address: getinfo@haworthpressinc.com].

Ruthann Robson
Photo by S. E. Valentine. Used by permission.

writer must write, which is a solitary activity requiring the forestalling of those who would claim one's time and attention. A dyke must disappoint others who had expectations that she would be heterosexual.

Selfishness has a bad reputation, of course. It's an accusation we level at others when we feel as if we're not getting our due. It's something we may worry over if we suspect it in ourselves. But, the selfishness I think of as negative is displayed by a narrow anxious self, what Freudians would call the ego. A writer's selfishness in those instances might be displayed when she worries over the placement of her work in an anthology or the misspelling of her name. A dyke's selfishness could be apparent when she finds herself resenting her lover's stories of a former lover. The self's anxiety–its "ish-ness"–concerns its felt necessity of proving its own importance.

But I want to argue for the significance of another kind of selfishness, call it capital "S" Selfishness. For the Self involved in this instance is the capital "S" Self. Forgetting the Freudians and their super-ego, I would prefer to think of this Self as being the drive to connect with something higher and more grandiose than daily life. Some call it Soul, or Spirit, or Goddess, or even God. And some do not name it at all. But practicing this kind of Selfishness paradoxically takes one out of that crabbed and insecure self which is prone to the kind of grasping selfishness we rightly abhor.

Too mystical for many, I suppose. Certainly not trendy in these postmodern times, when it is fashionable to reject any claims to truth or authenticity. Yet as a writer and a dyke, I feel I connect with something higher and more powerful when I engage in those selfish practices that make me a writer and a dyke. Meditation or ballet or pottery or tantric heterosexuality may work for others, but for me it's writing and sex. I like to think of these practices in broad senses; writing is not just pen to paper (or fingers to keyboard), just as sex is not just a finger on a clitoris. It's the idea scribbled and then crossed out; it's the flirtation; it's the car pulled over and pen pulled out to write a phrase; it's the kiss at the door goodbye and the smile hello. I might even call it a discipline. Working on a stanza because one word sounds wrong; looking at one's own body with love despite its scars. These practices forge a connection between the daily self and the expansive Self.

Not that I always connect. The struggle is to make that connection and to sustain it. This is not always easy, especially since the writer and the dyke are always in danger of being colonized–or in the term that I prefer, domesticated–by two other identities, that of the author and the lesbian.

Resisting the Author's domestication of the Writer is often difficult. It requires one to be Selfish. I strive to be Selfish by not allowing the Author much influence. It is the Author who looks at sales figures, who reads reviews, who gives readings and signs books and carefully considers the electronics rights clause in publishing contracts. These things may be necessary, but the Writer's Self must be protected against them lest they masquerade as the reasons the Writer writes. For I don't think the Writer writes to be an Author, she writes to explore some core of life that is otherwise inaccessible. Once the Writer concerns herself with sales figures or reviews of her last published effort, then the Writer's practice of her new work is affected. She might think of a reviewer's critique that a book did not have a happy ending, for example, and decide to have her new novel have a happy ending. When the impetus for writing comes from a desire to please others, the Writer is paradoxically locked inside her most parochial self.

Being Selfish as a Writer means writing for one's highest most expansive Self and exiling the Author. I have been heavily counseled to write about subjects and in genres other than the ones I am choosing. Replace poetry with a lesbian mystery, I've been told, by persons who believed they had my best interests at heart. Make my characters more likable, it's been suggested. Write shorter, write longer, take out the sex, pen erotica. The advice is often contradictory, but it consistently ignores the Self in favor of the market driven concerns that would interest the Author.

I try to write for my highest Self, but I often start my writing process with the ideas that interest my embodied lower case "s" self. I write things I want to know, but don't yet know when I start the writing. I write to solve a problem or explore an issue, even if that "issue" is one that I construct as a character, a plot, or a setting. For example, in the series of linked stories that is *Cecile,* I was occupied by the daily lives of two lesbians who were in love and stayed that way throughout the book. Until that time, I had not read a book involving a lesbian relationship that did not involve either a getting together love story or a breaking up/death tragedy. In the novel *Another Mother,* the situation I set for myself was a lesbian who was admired and cool and a professional role model on the outside and totally messed up on the inside. And in the novel *a/k/a,* I worried over whether there were such things as an essential core of identity and love at first sight.

Although fueled by lowercase "s" self-concerns, the actual practice of writing can lead to the concerns of this higher Self. For example, in *a/k/a,* my interest in the phenomenon of love at first sight led me to places that I could never have anticipated. In a novella entitled *Close to Utopia,* which will be part of my forthcoming collection of fiction, *The Struggle for Happiness,* I started with the issue of animal rights and found myself contemplating communication between animals and humans. Often, however, there is nothing in the content of the writing that reveals connection with the higher Self. For it is not really a matter of subject as much as it is a matter of the process, the practice, the craft. It's the juxtaposition of images, alliteration imagined or abandoned, a structural problem solved. It's listening to the chant-like sound of a line that no one else may hear or building the abstract scaffolding of a novel that will be invisible to most. It's sniffing out a word until it leaps out from behind the most unlikely bush, startling and almost scary.

Creative writing is most likely to manifest the epiphanies that mark connections with the higher Self, but I also try to practice Selfish Scholarship. Again, I strive to write about things that I want to know. What are the connections between the ways lesbians are treated in law and literature? How are lesbians treated when they are criminal defendants? How do critiques of narrative implicate lesbian narratives? What would happen if Sappho went to law school? Is it true that lesbians were never prosecuted for their sexual acts? In exploring these questions, I accessed what I thought were acceptable answers through the process of writing, supported by research and theorizing. As in fiction and poetry, however, I did not know what I wanted to say before I started the struggle to articulate it. Thus, I do not write to persuade or inform. I write because I want to know, even if what I want to know is only what I think about something.

I cannot always be Selfish, however, or even selfish. Like many others, writing is a part of the ways in which I earn a living. In my many years of working, as an attorney and a professor, I have written countless letters, more memos than I would like, a file cabinet full of exam hypotheticals and multiple choice questions, and probably hundreds of persuasive legal documents of all sorts. This type of writing is "work." Further, when asked, I do agree to do things that do not contribute to earning a living that I would classify as "service" rather than work or writing, such as encyclopedia entries, book reviews, and manuscript assessments. The Author rather than the Writer is asked to do these things and the Author rather than the Writer performs them. Nevertheless, I try to limit these activities and never allow the Author to write creatively. So when I am asked to submit a piece of erotica or a memoir or some science fiction, my possibility of submission is limited by pieces I have already written, even if only in draft.

My best writing–which may not be my most popular work or my most critically acclaimed work–occurs when my Self is caught making love with something higher than its self. Which brings me to the Selfishness of being a dyke.

Like the Writer in danger of being domesticated by the Author, the

Dyke lives in danger of being domesticated by the Lesbian. The Lesbian is the softer, more socially acceptable version, who struggles for the status of sexual subject in the context of political rights and who argues that her relationships are commensurate with heterosexual ones. The Lesbian is necessary, as is the Author, for she is the public figure whose goal is often to protect the private reality. Yet again, the inner Dyke needs to be protected from the outer Lesbian. The Lesbian would convince the Dyke that her reality is "equal" to heterosexuality. She would say that its ludicrous to believe that the practices of dykedom–whatever one believes them to be–come from some higher Self or connect with some higher Spirit.

I am not advocating that Writers or Dykes abandon the sensory or intellectual worlds in favor of some shapeless spirituality. In fact, I believe Writers and Dykes must live fully in these realms. The smell of ink and my lover's sweat. The logical structure of a paragraph and a discussion in bed with my lover. But these are not the only realms that are accessible to me as a Dyke and as a Writer. Not the only realms that surface in conversations with other Dykes and other Writers. Not the realms which cause me to be Selfish.

To be a Dyke Writer is to be Selfish. Being a Dyke is attempting to communicate with this capital "S" Self through the body. Being a Writer is attempting to communicate with this capital "S" Self through language. Yet both the body and language are ultimately inadequate. It's the fate–and the joy–of the Dyke Writer that we keep trying, in our Selfish determination and ambition, to get it right.

Mozart's Laugh

Jane Rule

Mozart's laugh, in the film *Amadeus,* is at first startlingly high and seems both silly and self-conscious. At the end of the film, after his death, that laugh is released, disembodied and angelic, a miracle like his music, transcending the little man, his little life and sad death. W.H. Auden wrote in "In Memory of W.B. Yeats," "You were silly like us; your gift survived it all."

Art, even our own, does not transform our lives. It does not cure Adrienne Rich's arthritis or Kate Millett's broken heart or Audre Lorde's cancer. But it does transcend the defining prisons of our suffering. We are silly; we die, and the song survives us.

Jane Rule
January 30, 1999

Jane Rule is a major, internationally recognized author. Her essays on literature are collected as *Lesbian Images* (Doubleday, Simon & Schuster, 1975, 1976), and *A Hot-Eyed Moderate* (Lester & Orpen Dennys, 1986). She is the author of many novels, including *After the Fire* (Pandora, Naiad, 1990, 1989), *Memory Board* (Pandora, Naiad, 1989, 1987), *Contract With the World* (Pandora, 1990, 1988), *The Young In One Another's Arms* (Pandora, 1990, 1977), *Against the Season* (P. Davies, 1971; Naiad, 1988), *This Is Not For You* (Pandora, 1990, 1970; Naiad, 1988), *Desert of the Heart* (Naiad, 1990, 1964). Collections of short stories are *Theme For Diverse Instruments* (Naiad, 1990), *Inland Passage and Other Stories* (Lester & Orpen, 1985), and *Outlander: Short Stories and Essays* (Naiad, 1981, 1982).
Address correspondence to: Jane Rule, RR #1, S19, C17, Galiano, British Columbia, Canada V0N 1P0.

[Haworth co-indexing entry note]: "Mozart's Laugh." Rule, Jane. Co-published simultaneously in *Journal of Lesbian Studies* (Harrington Park Press, an imprint of The Haworth Press, Inc.) Vol. 4, No. 4, 2000, pp. 131-132; and: *Lesbian Self-Writing: The Embodiment of Experience* (ed: Lynda Hall) Harrington Park Press, an imprint of The Haworth Press, Inc., 2000, pp. 131-132. Single or multiple copies of this article are available for a fee from The Haworth Document Delivery Service [1-800-342-9678, 9:00 a.m. - 5:00 p.m. (EST). E-mail address: getinfo@haworthpressinc.com].

Jane Rule
Photo by used by permission of the National Film Board of Canada.

A Truth of Being

Vanessa Scrivens

SUMMARY. In an exploration of what it means to write from a lesbian perspective, Vanessa Scrivens examines the process and the power of self-writing. She states that writing gives one the strength to give birth to the inner conscience and the courage to look it in the eye. A short piece of autobio/fictional writing that follows this discussion will hopefully give an example of the true potential that self-writing has. *[Article copies available for a fee from The Haworth Document Delivery Service: 1-800-342-9678. E-mail address: <getinfo@haworthpressinc.com> Website: <http://www.HaworthPress.com>]*

KEYWORDS. Lesbians, self-writing, child sexual abuse, memory, body

Writing, especially self-writing, has given me the chance to express myself when I would otherwise be mute. It lets me explore my true self and my desired state of being. When I put my pen to paper, I am free to speak my innermost thoughts and courageous enough to try to

---

Vanessa Scrivens is a self-proclaimed high school drop out who recently, at the age of twenty-three, finished her high school diploma. She is presently in her first year of studies at Mount Royal College in Calgary, Alberta. Her studies are in the field of Child and Youth Care, which will hopefully lead her toward her ultimate goal of a masters degree in counselling psychology. For several years she has worked in residential settings with children and youth. She is presently working in a group home for adolescents in Calgary. Working with children and youth is one of the many ways that she hopes to use her passion for writing in the future.

Address correspondence to: Vanessa Scrivens, 627 Sabrina Road S.W., Calgary, Alberta, Canada T2W 1Y7.

[Haworth co-indexing entry note]: "A Truth of Being." Scrivens, Vanessa. Co-published simultaneously in *Journal of Lesbian Studies* (Harrington Park Press, an imprint of The Haworth Press, Inc.) Vol. 4, No. 4, 2000, pp. 133-139; and: *Lesbian Self-Writing: The Embodiment of Experience* (ed: Lynda Hall) Harrington Park Press, an imprint of The Haworth Press, Inc., 2000, pp. 133-139. Single or multiple copies of this article are available for a fee from The Haworth Document Delivery Service [1-800-342-9678, 9:00 a.m. - 5:00 p.m. (EST). E-mail address: getinfo@haworthpressinc.com].

Vanessa Scrivens
Photo by Tara Scrivens. Used by permission.

build safe places to do so. Through writing I have learned much about myself, about lesbian writing, and about how my own sexuality affects my writing. The topics I write about and the content that I include in my written self-expression are diverse. Different types of writing have served different purposes in my life.

I began writing stories about women loving other women for the sole purpose of providing myself with reading material that related to my life. It hasn't taken me a long time to realize that the pleasure I take in what I write is not in the reading of it. I revel in the power that writing gives me to explore my thoughts, my dreams, and my past. At times, writing provides me with the strength to give birth to my inner conscience and the courage to actually look it in the eye.

As a young girl in elementary school, I wrote stories of secret clubs for girls. There were always aspects of true closeness between the female characters in the stories and an underlying respect for the unity and secretiveness of the clubs themselves. As I grew older, my writing matured with me. Soon the secret handshakes were replaced with knowing glances and stolen kisses. When I became old enough to gain access to women's bars, my stories evolved again. Surprisingly, or maybe not, there is a tremendous similarity between the relationships and the atmosphere in what I refer to as my secret club stories and the experiences I wrote about within the bar scene.

My stories, poems, and scribbled ideas are an accurate log of my life. They give me sources of reference to my own history. As I look through the words that I have chosen to put to paper in the past, I am able to see the amount of growth in my life. My shoe box and file folder memories are overflowing with records of loved ones that now exist only in my depictions of them, fears and fantasies stored safely in sealed envelopes, and lovers from my past and my present reality. Whether or not they appear in their true form, by their real names, or in contexts in which I truly knew them, all of the people I care about are with me always in my writing. Even when I write of myself, they are there standing unobtrusively behind me, encouraging me to give voice to my experiences and to my reality.

For many years after I came to terms with my sexuality, I wrote only about my experiences as a lesbian. I thought that I had to scream to the world that I loved other women and that I would no longer be willing to live in the box that social ignorance had built for me. Now, I have realized that by focussing only on my sexuality, I was in fact building myself a box which would become inescapable until I could stop neglecting other facets of my personality and of my life. I refuse to allow myself to be defined by who I prefer to spend my intimate life with. I would not permit anyone else to classify me this way. I refuse to label myself in that manner, because by doing so I completely invalidate all of the other factors that shape who I am.

I now realize that no matter what the content of my written words, they come from a lesbian perspective. When I write about housework, religion, travelling, or even about a breath-taking sunset, it is all from this perspective. It would be impossible for me to speak of anything without coming from this viewpoint, simply because no matter what I am doing, or where I am, I am myself. That self (or selves) is always a lesbian.

The people in my life who really care about me have never asked me to write only of my life as a lesbian, nor have they asked me to silence this part of my self-expression. They respect that writing, in any form, is an intimate process. I think my process of writing is as personal and private as getting dressed. Both before going out and while I am writing, I must find some way to define myself.

When clothing myself I choose colours and fabrics that will guard me from the elements and ultimately define me for the day. Contrarily, when I write I choose to stay in my most natural form and exposed to all of the elements of the world. I have a need to be free to experience my life. I choose to define myself and keep myself warm with the words that seep from my mind and spirit. Gently, they will float down and wrap themselves around my body, covering me with their meaning, then they slide away again. Alone in the dark, I stand naked, waiting with anticipation for the next word or phrase that will shed light on me.

Much of my written word has enlightened me about my own experiences and my perception of my life. Two pieces, in particular, have had a significant impact on my life. The first is a short poem entitled "Dear Mr. Christie" that I wrote several years ago. While I wasn't aware of the truth it spoke when I originally wrote it, I now see that there is no coincidence that it was written at a time in my life when I was trying to deal with issues of sexual abuse from my past. At the time that this poem was written, I was also just beginning to come to terms with my own sexuality.

> *Dear Mr. Christie,*
> *I am the cookie who crumbled*
> *You held me too tightly, too long*
> *Your ravenous appetite and your half-baked ideas*
> *Broke my spirit, my body, my sweetness*
> *shall never touch your lips*
> *or satisfy your insatiable hunger . . .*
> *again.*

Through writing this poem, and rereading it, I began to feel that I had regained a sense of control over my body and my life. Every word that is written reveals and frees a secret that I no longer feel responsible for. A great part of the pleasure I have in writing is that no one can have power over what I write. While some people might not like what I have to say, they cannot stop me from saying it, nor can they deny that it has been said. Once my inner voice, a pen, and a piece of paper have become intimately entwined, there is no separating them. Once penned, my words can sprout wings to guide them out of their confines and into the realm of the collective unconscious. Perhaps it is ironic that I write of control and also of freedom, but I believe that freedom and control are mirror images of one another.

The second piece of writing that I find particularly relevant to my life also addresses my need for control over myself, and my wish to free my mind from the confusion of reality. Although I speak only of my perspective of painting my world and my self, this piece is also relevant to my writing and rewriting of my self. Both painting and writing provide my thoughts and feelings with tangible outlets of expression. Likewise, both forms of expression are tools for self-creation and understanding.

Many forms of self-expression allow me to free what is trapped inside my soul and inside my mind. They permit me to put my fears and my fantasies on paper, examine them carefully, patiently dissect them to see all of the beauty and the ugliness that exists within them, and then rob them of their pelts to use as their own title. I find that it is easiest to remove the outside barriers, and then examine the inner framework and the foundation. The following is an example of how art, specifically painting, allows me to create what I believe is lacking in my life and also re-create the aspects of myself that I am unhappy with.

A Painted Affair

The night is devoid of all meaning; the silence sits heavily on my mind. As I wander aimlessly through my home, I come across the broken mirror that hangs from my bathroom door. The reflection speaks of truths and fallacies that I am uninterested in hearing. I am unhappy with, and scared of, my own image. I must create a self that pleases me. I must be in charge of designing the person I believe myself to be. Nothing helps me to do this better than a bottle of wine (preferably a blush) and a full spectrum of paint.

In the silence, all that can be heard is the gentle sigh of each jar of paint as their lids are carefully removed. Their breath becomes mine as the chalky, sweetness of the air fills my lungs. I inhale the passion of the yellow and red, exhaling an exhilarating breath of orange. Slowly, blue seeps out of its jar and blankets me in calmness that is undefinable. Each in turn, the colors dance toward me and stir within me. As I squat precariously over a large canvas, containers of paint erupt. The paint pools, like teardrops shed from a prism. I delight in the sensation of the cool, wet consistency between my toes.

I am not a tidy painter. Tonight is a fine example of this. I have begun to blend colors and shapes across the canvas. My body and my mind are liberated by the control I possess over each new creation. The paint is so thick and moist that I am capable of manipulating and changing its form long after I first create it. Nothing pleases me more than to be completely enmeshed in my own creation. As usual, I have left my brushes stored safely in their pristine case. In my periphery I can see them mocking my childlike exuberance.

With paint covering my arms, I can truly feel the power of my own fingers and the paint itself. A bottle of wine has freed my mind, allowing me to become my own creator. As the paint touches my skin it warms and dries. It is as if I am cocooning myself in rainbow armour. I feel very infantile in my process. I allow myself to only know my world in a sensual way.

Eventually, the paint begins to fall from my body and the alcohol to fall from my mind. My world has begun to appear mundane and washed out again. Instead of the vibrant and lively acrylic vision I had, I see in soft watercolour shades that bore me incessantly. Even the soap bubbles I use to clean up the remnants of my self-portrait are filled with pastel shades of sleepy colors. I weep as I wipe up my rainbow dream.

No matter how I choose to create myself, or how often I choose to redefine what has already been created, there is a community of people who acknowledge and validate the person I have become. They are aware that I, like them, am constantly evolving and finding new meaning in who I am. It is often this group of individuals who serve as an impetus for change in my life. When reading my short stories or poetry, or upon viewing one of my paintings or sketches, they can also bring meaning out of images constructed unconsciously. Through their interpretations, they bear witness to many experiences that have ostracized me from reality in the past.

I credit a great deal of my willingness to explore myself to the many people who have come into my life and touched my heart. These people include my family (biological and chosen), my instructors (past and present), and especially my partner, Tara. All of these individuals have encouraged me to challenge and examine who I am. Without them, it is unlikely that I would have the courage or the confidence to look at, never mind share, the often-frightening images that my mind vomits onto paper.

The Unfinished Moon

Betsy Warland

SUMMARY. The author explores several questions. She asks: What does it mean to exist as a lesbian writer given that we have no lesbian homeland or ancestral tongue, little presence in the external narrative matrix, a scarcity of close friendships among ourselves, a lack of contact with younger lesbian writers, and an erasure of our lesbianism due to heterosexuals relating to us as "single" women in the literary community? If the intense individuation processes of establishing our lesbian identities are what we share more than our diverse lifestyles as lesbians–how do we enable a feminist-lesbian literary community and tradition to flourish? *[Article copies available for a fee from The Haworth Document Delivery Service: 1-800-342-9678. E-mail address: <getinfo@haworthpressinc.com> Website: <http://www.HaworthPress.com>]*

KEYWORDS. Lesbian, individuation, self-writing, narrative, collective presence, publishing

A lesbian writer is like no other writer.

The lesbian writer has no lesbian homeland.

What Holds Us Here, Betsy Warland's collection of nine suites of poems, was published in 1998, and her ninth book, *Bloodroot–Tracing the Untelling of Motherloss* (prose), in 2000. She initiated and co-coordinated the *Women and Words/Les femmes et les mots* Canadian/Quebec conference in 1983, co-edited *Telling It: Women and Language Across Cultures* (1990), and edited *Inversions: Writing by Dykes, Queers, and Lesbians* (1991).

Address correspondence to: Betsy Warland, 45 Havelock Street, Toronto, Ontario, Canada M6H 3B3.

[Haworth co-indexing entry note]: "The Unfinished Moon." Warland, Betsy. Co-published simultaneously in *Journal of Lesbian Studies* (Harrington Park Press, an imprint of The Haworth Press, Inc.) Vol. 4, No. 4, 2000, pp. 141-148; and: *Lesbian Self-Writing: The Embodiment of Experience* (ed: Lynda Hall) Harrington Park Press, an imprint of The Haworth Press, Inc., 2000, pp. 141-148. Single or multiple copies of this article are available for a fee from The Haworth Document Delivery Service [1-800-342-9678, 9:00 a.m.–5:00 p.m. (EST). E-mail address: getinfo@haworthpressinc.com].

Betsy Warland
Photo by Susan Shantz. Used by permission.

Not even an ancestral homeland from which she or her ancestors have been separated. A fictional lesbian utopia is as close as she comes.

The lesbian writer has no ancestral lesbian tongue.

She may listen imaginatively to Sappho's shards of lyrics. She may read between the lines of Emily Dickinson's love poems but she must teach herself her own use of language while she navigates hatred toward her embedded in that very language; while she ignores prevailing dogma asserting that her culture does not exist because it lacks its own language.

The lesbian writer has no external narrative* matrix.

Her narrative throbs within her body. When she looks out into the world she rarely finds evidence of her existence. She is a character who must write her own play.

The external narrative matrix supports a wide range of narratives that differ from, depend upon, and reference one another. Yet these disparate narratives are not so disparate when it comes to their representation of sexuality which is almost exclusively heterosexual.

For a new generative source of narratives to successfully enter the external narrative matrix two operative factors seem crucial. First, that these new narratives claim their particular relationship with the matrix. Second, that the writers of these new narratives form an identifiable collective presence and impetus.

This has happened, for example, with Afro-American writers, who draw upon remembered and sensed fragments of their nearly obliterated ancestral narratives/histories/languages (their collective presence) as well as their mutual experience of slavery in the United States (their relationship with the matrix).

With the establishment of relationship with the external matrix–new narratives assert the larger truth of our society's lived experience: we are not all heterosexual, middle class, stereotypically-gendered people of European descent.

To me, the existence and vitality of Canadian lesbian new narratives seem apparent. There are a number of us who have written books in which our feminist-lesbian sensualities, unauthorized experiences, and rogue (as in wave) perceptions create new, supple, forms; inventive language; and unpredictable narratives.

The extent to which our new narratives have established their relationship to the matrix is less certain. In part, this is due to ourselves, for the existence of what we share as Canadian lesbian writers (our collective presence) is sporadically established among ourselves, and as a result, far less apparent to the literary community.

> To be a lesbian, each of us has had to painfully assert our separateness.

Unlike membership in almost any other minority group, we are not born into lesbianism: our minority status is not an automatic racial or cultural given. Nor is our minority status inevitable with the passage of time–like the elderly. Nor is our minority status a result of circumstance being thrust upon us–like the physically or mentally challenged.

We lesbians exist only as a result of our own profound individuation processes. To exist as a lesbian, each of us has had to painfully assert our difference and separateness from our heterosexual (and most often homophobic) family and community of origin.

What we "share" as lesbians may be the intensity of our individuation experiences more than our diverse lesbian lifestyles. Ironically, this necessary separation process may be the very thing that impedes us from actively nourishing our identifiable collective presence. Our trust may be stalled with our relinquishment of being deeply part of our early primary groups of family and community.

Among lesbian writers there is a scarcity of close friendships.

We are often too scattered geographically to enjoy close companionship with one another. Lesbian writers are also very diverse and consequently, we tend to be cautious with one another.

How then does the lesbian writer exist?

Exist, ex -, ***out*** *+ sistere, to take a* ***position, stand firm****?*

What is she birthed *out* of?
What *position* does she take?
Upon what might she *stand firm*?

She is birthed out of absence.
She is Other.
She floats.

In order to "float," the elements or mediums in which you work as a writer must support you (not be hostile toward you). We lesbian writers employ many different strategies through which we establish a creative environment that sustains and stimulates us. During my first number of writing years, I focused on decoding, reclaiming, and re-configuring the English language along with the erotic language of the lesbian body (*open is broken,* 1984; *serpent (w)rite,* 1987; *Double Negative,* 1988; *Proper Deafinitons,* 1990). As my integrity and imagination in these flourished, I turned more toward investigating personal history and Western society's assumptions and notions about narrative itself (*The Bat Had Blue Eyes,* 1993; *What Holds Us Here,* 1997; *Bloodroot,* 2000).

Whether the experience of inhabiting my lesbian body has been a topic of love poems, a lens through which I exposed the mono-versions of familial, Western, or Judeo-Christian beliefs and histories, or the unorthodox site from which I companioned and later wrote about my dying mother, writing from my lesbian body has been a consistent source.

There is the lesbian body plural (which is of most interest to me in this essay); the lesbian body coupled; the lesbian body singular. For me, the lesbian body singular and self writing are almost synonymous. "Other" is what is between "absence" and "presence": it is absence activated. To evoke reality there must be tangible, compelling bodies and identities. As each lesbian writer finds her own way to float, her writing requires her readers to do the same, for her readers must negotiate not only her activated absences but, in some sense, their own forms of absence–no matter how different or denied. For this reason many readers (including most lesbians) never open our books. Readers who do, frequently experience a surprising range of intense reactions from anger to disorientation to enthrallment.

To read a book is an act of surrender.

When we readers choose to read any book–we give ourselves to that book. Absorb the book's words into our hearts, bodies, minds. Reading is an intimate act. It requires our embrace of trust and curiosity. The more a writer resides within the authorized, external narrative matrix–the more automatic, even unthinking, this embrace is. The less a writer resides within the external narrative matrix–the less automatic, more debated it is.

To be embraced you must have a face.

Whether as writer, reader, or book–to be embraced you must have a face. Readers need to be aware of a book in order to make a decision to read it. In Canada, most often the reader's embrace is prompted by the literary canon. The canon is maintained by academic institutions which, in turn, frequently influence which books get published and reviewed. The academy is also the official trainer of young writers.

Aggressive marketing of a book attracts readers but again, in Canada, this marketing often rides on academic literary trends such as post-modernism and post-colonialism.

Corporate mega bookstores, whose marketing rides on popular culture's trends, also shape sales, but less so in Canada due to our small national population. Whether canon or corporate, heterosexual-based connections and sensibilities are the foundation of the North American book industry.

Beyond the heterosexual-based book industry, the reader's embrace can also be facilitated for those lesbian writers who write for a popular lesbian readership. Again, in Canada, this proves to be a limited readership due to our small population. Compounding this are the severe government funding cutbacks of the '90s which have significantly limited or eliminated feminist-lesbian run (or lesbian-positive) publishers, periodicals, literary events, and writing workshops.

Our '80s Canadian dream of a feminist and feminist-lesbian literary movement in which we assumed our own authority for unleashing our full potential in the production and promotion of lesbian books has not been realized. I experience far fewer options as a feminist-lesbian writer today than I did 10 years ago. Excepting the tenacious feminist-lesbian and feminist presses which have survived–the decisions concerning who and what gets published and perhaps more crucially, promoted, remains largely in the hands of heterosexual men.

The lesbian writer: a "single" woman in the literary community.

In Canada, lesbian writers must be perceived as single women. "Unavailable," yet nevertheless familiar in heterosexual terms. The Canadian lesbian writer may have a known partner, may write about lesbian intimacy, but her private life must remain more of a fiction than a reality. Granted, the maintaining of one's private life as more of a fiction than a reality may be the preference for some lesbian writers. The point is–that regardless of our personal preferences–we have no choice in the matter.

The target of homophobia, when directed at lesbians, is often the lesbian couple. Lesbians are not a visible minority nor a geographically-based community; consequently, without the couple, we can easily be redefined into "single" women by non-gays. Treating the lesbian couple divisively (excluding one while including the other) is one form of heterosexualizing us into "single" women.

Although there are literary gay men, as well as non-homophobic heterosexual women and men, who are some of our most perceptive readers, the Canadian literary community's collective instincts are homophobic.

Continuing to open the sky.

We are at a very young and crucial point in the creation of our feminist-lesbian literary tradition. If, in Canada, we are to become less dependent upon heterosexual endorsement of our work, it is imperative that we enter the external narrative matrix more on our own terms. We need to be a more identifiable, energetic presence: lesbian writers in the plural. And, we need to help one another professionally more (as fellow writers routinely do) and be less concerned about being perceived as "a bunch of lesbians."

Otherwise, we will essentially remain politely (in most cases) distant from one another. We will continue to be isolated from younger generations of lesbian writers, particularly those not associated with the academy. I find the young lesbian writers I work with adrift. They are isolated from one another. And they are isolated from us–their potential mentors. They deeply feel the lack of a feminist-lesbian literary community. It is time to create more opportunities for talented young lesbian writers. A simple way of doing this is for us to step aside from time to time–as we have seen established First Nations writers do for young First Nations writers–pass on some of our professional invitations to them; showcase them in our readings and writings.

In the midst of writing this I awoke one night saying 'the unfinished moon.' With the exception of a handful of nights a year, the moon appears to exist in various stages of being 'unfinished.' It is easy to forget that it is, in fact, always full. With the enabling of one another we enable ourselves. We are not on a quota system. Sharing our power as a writer and professional only creates more power for lesbian writers in general.

Without a doubt, among ourselves we are an unruly lot. Our dissimilarities are so vast that the phrase "lesbian writers" sometimes seems meaningless. Yet, here we are–writing for this anthology. After a decade or two of facing into our differences of race, class, and ideology, there are still core experiences we continue to recognize and respect in one another. We do not erase one another's lesbianism. Most often, we do not belittle it. We do not have to explain or defend our lesbianism as a significant source of our being and creativity.

We know what it meant to us when the sky was first opened by Lorde, Rich, Brossard, Daly, Cixous, Millett, Rule, Walker, Wittig, Sarton, Broumas, Grahn . . .

We are lesbian writers: we cannot be "normalized."

Despite our other primary names as writers, women, and human beings. Despite our real, often profound differences. Despite that we, in fact, frequently write about other topics. Despite our range of literary styles, personal and professional histories. Despite that for many of us–lesbians do not comprise the majority of our readers.

It is an odd *position.* Complex. Intense. Fluid. Familiar.

> We are birthed out of absence.
> We are Other.
> We float.

* In this essay I am using the term narrative as an inclusive term representing all genres of writing.

Why Writers Make Lousy Lovers

Jess Wells

SUMMARY. Jess Wells takes a light-hearted look at the pit-falls of being in love with a writer, describing the difficulties with time and reality. Wells then encourages lesbian authors to develop diversity among their art forms, income and inspiration sources. She wraps up with a call for lesbian writers to cultivate discipline and gratitude. *[Article copies available for a fee from The Haworth Document Delivery Service: 1-800-342-9678. E-mail address: <getinfo@haworthpressinc.com> Website: <http://www.HaworthPress.com>]*

KEYWORDS. Lesbians, self-writing, lesbian relationships, publishing, time

My ex-wife swears she'll never marry another writer–and while it may just be post-divorce self-esteem problems–I can't say I blame her. We are an unreliable lot.

Ignore for a moment the amount of solitude writers require, how we

---

Jess Wells' ten volumes of work include the new novel *The Price of Passion* (Firebrand Books, 1999). Her previous novel, *AfterShocks* (Third Side Press, U.S., 1992, The Women's Press, U.K., 1993), was nominated for the American Library Association Gay and Lesbian Literary Award. The anthology *Lesbians Raising Sons* (Alyson Publications, 1997) was a finalist for a Lambda Literary Award. Her five collections of short stories include *Loon Lake Duet* (currently seeking publication), *Two Willow Chairs* (Library B/Third Side Press, 1987), and *The Dress/The Sharda Stories* (Library B/Third Side Press, 1986).

Address correspondence to: Jess Wells, 93 Sequoia Way, San Francisco, CA 94127 USA.

[Haworth co-indexing entry note]: "Why Writers Make Lousy Lovers." Jess Wells. Co-published simultaneously in *Journal of Lesbian Studies* (Harrington Park Press, an imprint of The Haworth Press, Inc.) Vol. 4, No. 4, 2000, pp. 149-157; and: *Lesbian Self-Writing: The Embodiment of Experience* (ed: Lynda Hall) Harrington Park Press, an imprint of The Haworth Press, Inc., 2000, pp. 149-157. Single or multiple copies of this article are available for a fee from The Haworth Document Delivery Service [1-800-342-9678, 9:00 a.m. - 5:00 p.m. (EST). E-mail address: getinfo@haworthpressinc.com].

Jess Wells
Photo by Rick Bolen. Used by permission.

insist on the best room with the best light for our offices, how we ditch out on parties and trips to the in-laws for a chance to work on our novels, how we suddenly get an idea and get out of bed or refuse to go out, even though we're dressed with tickets in our hand. The real problem is that we are frequently only partially there when we're there. Driving, we daydream. My ex was finally trained to ask, "are you writing?" when she wanted to talk about our dog-food shortage, but looked to the passenger side and found me in (my favorite) trance-like state.

The lover of a writer has to understand that we are chemically different than other people. You see, beta states are for linear thought; alpha waves are for creative thought; and theta waves are deep sleep.

As a writer, it is a physiological/chemical requirement that we live a certain number of hours each day or each week in the alpha state. When the world insists that we are in beta too much, not able to dream or to write, it's a chemical deprivation. One of my ex-lovers, coming through the door to the smell of a delicious home-cooked meal, the apartment vacuumed and tidied, would put down her tool belt and glumly say, "bad day writing, Jess?" She knew it had been a day of too much beta.

The lover of a writer is almost non-monogamous by default. She has to accept the fact that a writer has an entirely separate world going on in her head that is populated by fascinating people about whom she cares deeply, controls utterly, and ponders incessantly. She has up to two dozen people whose backgrounds, physicality, motivations, and emotional growth are of paramount importance to her. A writer lives on at least two different planes, the physical one she's in and the one she's inventing.

The physical plane is a much more difficult place for me, because I'm a writer. Ignoring the fact that a large portion of my money goes to writer-type equipment and activities, and that I believe that the best thing money can buy is time for not making money, I have trouble with the basic linearity of life–the time and space of it. Like most writers, I have tried hard to cultivate the ability to really feel on a gut level many things and experiences that I haven't actually lived through. Sitting at my desk, I feel cool water against my skin the way my character does as she's skinny-dipping at midnight. This ability to feel what isn't real is one I have cultivated for years. As a child, I used to ride in the car with my palm against the window, trying to call into my hands the feel of each leaf, tree bark, light pole, dog fur, house siding that I passed. I got good enough at it that on the train back and forth to college the sensations would flow into my hand in a stream that picked up pace and raced into my mind. It's a good technique for writers. Our job is to break through the barrier between concept and physical sensation, past and present. For a writer, to think it, is to feel it. Our sense of reality must be permeable, mutable. We dwell in what isn't and our success depends upon our being able to experience what we haven't, to call up events from the past and re-live them, to synthesize the experiences of many and bring them so close that we can feel them on our skin. We don't just live in our minds, in a world of unreality, we bring that unreality into our bodies, our fingertips, the palms of our hands, the pit of our stomachs.

But as a partner, this tendency makes us somewhat undependable. How do you build a life with someone who actively cultivates a tenuous grip on reality? When my ex would say "have you seen that blue envelope?" the answer would have to be yes. Envelope, blue, sure. As soon as she says it, I feel it. I've seen it on one plane or another. "Was it there yesterday?" Well, now I'm completely screwed because she's introduced another layer of linearity. Time. That's the hardest one for me. "Did you give the dog her pills?" I can see it. Dog's throat, little white pills. I can feel her lips on my fingers. Yes, I did. "Did you give them to her yesterday morning and last night?" Now, morning and evening feel palpably different so I can tell them apart, but *yesterday* morning? Which morning, I don't know. Some morning, the dog got her pills.

So we nurture a group of intimates who don't exist. We purposely detach ourselves from reality, cultivate a physical presence with things we can't touch, dream when others would be thinking, think when others would be doing. And we lie. Writers will say anything that is well said. One-liners about ourselves that are exaggerations. Embellished stories that make our lovers seem funnier, fatter, more stupid, more selfless or self-absorbed, more a victim, more a champion. Truth gives way to the well-turned phrase.

And we steal. We tell other people's stories, we boil our friends down to amalgamated characters, we walk off with the gestures of people in the street. If we don't consciously develop a personal code of ethics, writers can turn everything and everyone into fodder for our fiction.

Now, let's ignore for a moment the fact that writers are intense people with overblown emotions that are vociferously stated (because the process of writing dilutes everything, really. Passion that starts at a very high level translates onto paper as mild interest). Let's ignore the fact that writers are subject to mood swings depending on our ability to translate the world in our head onto paper, and that we frequently blame our lovers for an emptiness in our lives that can only be filled by our imaginary characters and the time we allow them to come alive. If you're going to be the lover of a writer, I say memorize the protagonist's name and when your adored writer demands more of you, tell her to get it off the protagonist.

Which is not to say that you shouldn't honor the writer's dilemma, which is in some ways inherent to the art form and in some ways symptomatic of the arts in America. Writing is extremely solitary and yet writers are driven to external reward and fame, perhaps only a notch down from actresses. And writers are terribly undervalued, judged by book sales and money which has little to do with art, and so they struggle with a type of schizophrenia working day jobs.

The communication issues are the real ones that astound me with regards to writers. We are a font of ideas, completely disinterested in the implementation, practicality or budgeting issues related to the ideas. They come in an endless stream, like a six year old with finger paints. What if we did that? What if we changed it this way? Wouldn't it be funny if we . . . ? I honestly tell you (no embellishment here) that I didn't think to teach my wife to greet my ideas with the retort "interesting material, Jess. You'll have to use that somewhere" before I had completely exhausted her with my deluge of ideas. She had made the mistake of taking me seriously and judged me to be, shall we say, tediously inventive.

I had ruined my credibility, which was further damaged by my mistake of telling my ex that I talk to myself so much, and have so many internal dialogues that at times I don't really know if I have spoken out loud. Now, that doesn't seem odd to another writer, because we know the amount of time and energy spent on trying out dialogue, refining a line, thinking up plot lines, developing that internal world. But to a partner who wants to know why she didn't know that the dinner date had been moved to another restaurant, this internal dialogue seems to be a problem. You can swear up and down that you know that you have to verbalize when the information pertains to that foreign soil called reality, but once your lover knows you're confused by the linear plane, you're sunk.

My ex is now dating an accountant (well, that's an embellishment). And me? Did I say out loud that I was single again?

I have an electronic post-it note on my computer, a quote from an Agatha Christie movie: "Artists: they never know whether to kill themselves or throw a party." If you're interested in being published, or in advancing where and when you're published, I say welcome to the swing between suicide and celebration. It's an emotionally taxing life. It's a gratifying life. It's a life we should be thankful we have, in a world when so few have any passion for what they do. But be forewarned that especially as lesbian authors there is less money in it than for almost anyone on the planet; there are fewer publishing venues than for almost anyone on the planet; and there are appalling inequities in the opportunities and the money given to lesbians and gay men.

Especially for lesbian authors, the concept of diversity has become a watchword. We need to honor a diversity of publishing venues because we have so few. We need to survive with a diversity of lives because we have so little money. We have the wonderful opportunity to thrive and create with diversity because we're formulating a body of literature that hasn't been seen before, for a culture that is coming out of the shadows.

It's important to know that even publishing is not all about books and paper. Writers who are successful are also good performers. An entertaining, engaging reading is one of the best, or certainly most prevalent, ways of promoting your book. It's very helpful to study with a drama coach, and to take workshops on one-woman shows, in performance art. And not just for the reading of the written word; an improvisation class can get you in touch with voices that you didn't know you had inside you, voices that can then become characters. Nina Wise teaches here in the Bay Area and one of her exercises at the beginning of class was to lay on the floor and make the most obnoxious noise you could come up with. It was very liberating, and the more you are liberated from the confines of linear thought, the better your writing.

Learn to sing; write about a singer; write with tonality and rhythm. Learn to dance; write about movement; infuse your writing with the images of sweat and muscles and internal inspiration. Because your metaphors don't come from books. You can't write about reading or writing, about sitting on the couch in your old pajamas turning the pages of a book. You can write about the couch, the pajamas, the sitting, but not the reading. So if the book is off limits, your metaphors have to come from somewhere else.

I suggest you diversify the place where you think. Not just here between your eyes (linear thought), and the top of your head (inspiration), but in your solar plexus, your heart, your throat, your survival chakra, the end points of your hands and feet. Get in touch; listen to what they have to say. Constantly come up with a variety of ways to burn new neural pathways, and new ways to find ideas that are growing in the edges of your mind, in the tissues of your body.

Look into a diversity of genres–short story, a novella, an anthology, an essay. Switching between them keeps your mind sharp. Different ideas demand different genres and you may even try two or three before the right medium presents itself. Cultivate diversity in other ways: what about another time zone? another planet? what about history? what about your own past lives? a different gender?

As to the publishing world itself, I suggest honoring all the diversity that's there, including: anthologies, magazines, small press, straight press, queer press, feminist, big, corporate, and university press. Honor it all, because it's all necessary. And because the place you thought was too small or too queer or too corporate or too smutty is exactly the place where you're going to have to humbly ask to publish you next month.

Expanding your concept of time is important as a lesbian writer, especially when it comes to publishing. The very fine author Jennifer Levin once said that she doesn't worry about how many years it takes her to write a book. She measures her writing career in a time-frame that is beyond her own physical life: we're building a body of literature for the lesbian community and notoriety is so tied up with our civil rights and growth as a culture that it can't be measured in one lifetime. She's looking to move forward the entire body of her work. Not just little blips of celebration. I imagine that she is describing the difference between being an actress and being a celebrity. You become a celebrity by paying attention to the publishing, but not the work.

Which is not to say that you shouldn't be disciplined about actively pursuing publication. I am always surprised when I meet people who are very organized and driven at their jobs, but then don't apply any of those practices to writing and being published. I have a calendar of anthology deadlines to meet on the wall next to my keyboard and I mark the dates when I send the manuscripts out. It's a way of charting output. I count how many submissions I've made each year. I highlight the ones I get into as a form of celebration. I actually record in my calendar how many hours each day I work for money and how many hours I work on fiction. If I fall below my goal (which is about 80 hours a month), I know it, adjust the following month's schedule. I cattle-prod myself with goals, like shortening the time between novels; like annual literary goals that I keep on my altar and consult every few months to see if I'm moving ahead; a list of editors to get to know; events where I need to be present; manuscripts that I want to finish before a particular holiday. Subscribe to *Poets and Writers* and submit to anthologies. Submit to the literary journals that we have left. Keep looking for venues, online and print. Read at open mikes. Be professional. Show up at readings, be respectful to other writers, re-write based on how it sounded at the reading. Be cooperative with editors wherever and whenever you find them, and if you can't find them, hire them privately. It is absolutely worth the money. Hire a private editor, set deadlines for yourself, be disciplined, be humble. Spend twice as much time and energy at being good as you do at being noticed. Work your craft.

It is difficult to honor the alpha-wave lifestyle. Setting up a lifestyle to honor that mixture is difficult. Especially as lesbian authors. We are forced into a level of diversity (alpha/beta; day-job/art-work) that others are not. If they're not going to pay us for our writing–with fewer grants, fewer stipends, and fewer publishing opportunities–we've got to have day jobs longer than anyone else, for more hours than anyone else, and that is compounded by the fact that as women we make less than fifty-two cents on the dollar. Thriving within that diversity is critical for us.

I can honestly say that the publishing industry has driven me to Buddhism. (And the state of the industry these days is making me increasingly devout.) Buddhism has given me the example of recognizing that in every moment there is the potential for joy. Even when you get rejected by the anthology editors, when you feel lost in the vortex of a novel, when that spectacular, lush, complicated world in your head gets down on paper and feels so flat, when that agent that you hung your hopes on calls to say "great work gal but I can't take you." I have friends who have threatened to fly cross country to slap me silly until I remember this, but it's not the publishing, it's the work. It's not the destination, it's the journey. It's the balance between sharing your work, which means publishing, and doing your work, which is the writing. From growing your craft, versus focusing solely on growing the stature of the publishing venues you're in. There's a big difference, and it's damn hard to remember. Where is the model of healthy ambition? Of wanting to achieve, and working damn hard, but remembering that you are not your work. That you have a life, not just a career.

After you write for a few years you know that you are a storyteller. The facts come from reality, history, from the dialogue and lives of you and your friends. From TV shows and bits of vacations. If you think you invent your ideas, rather than channel ideas, you can become afraid that you're going to dry up, and run out of material. As a writer, you are a conduit for the stories of the world. And as a published writer, whether you're conducting the lights of Broadway or the night-light in your three-year-old's room is not really for you to know. It's for you just to be thankful that you're the pipe for the goddess's pipe dream.

There's a terrific Buddhist prayer that seems just right for the thirst for publishing fame that infects us. A drop of water on the beach feels so terribly inadequate, so much the underachiever. "I must get to the sea, I must get to the sea," it wails. And the ocean replies, "you are the wave." You are the sea because you are the wave. You are a published author. You're already there.

Essential to this understanding is a sense of gratitude. Gratitude for each time your name is in print. Whether it's on a marquee or a mimeograph, it is essential that we celebrate our good fortune, our opportunity to share, and have gratitude for the world's willingness to listen to us.

And so I wish for you great publishing venues, increased circulation, royalties and reviews and your name on the spine. Most of all I wish for you an endless journey of stories that push you to your limit, hone you at your craft, and fill you with gratification.

Nobody Ever Asked Me
If I Had an Agent

Mary Wings

SUMMARY. There are many ways to write about/think about how I became an author. I like to think I chose this way because I had a 'hidden talent' that was brought forth by being in another country. This story could also be the story of a divorce, a yearning for adventure, the love of a genre, the quest for identity. I like to tell the story in this way because I like the idea that we all have hidden talents that are revealed by circumstance. And I like to urge people to do radical things. *[Article copies available for a fee from The Haworth Document Delivery Service: 1-800-342-9678. E-mail address: <getinfo@haworthpressinc.com> Website: <http://www.HaworthPress.com>]*

KEYWORDS. Lesbians, self-writing, family, lesbian relationships, publishing

My writing life, as I have lived it, seems to have defied all the clichés and conventional wisdom about writing. Writing started out as an amusement, a necessary diversion and eventually a job.

Mary Wings has written six novels: *She Came in Drag, She Came to the Castro, She Came by the Book, Divine Victim, She Came in a Flash,* and *She Came Too Late.* Winner of the Lambda Literary Award (*Divine Victim*), Wings was also short-listed for the Raymond Chandler Fulbright. She lives in San Francisco with two cats and a Shetland Sheepdog. She writes for radio, ghosts, and wishes she had more time to paint. Someday she will write *She Came for Christmas.*

Address correspondence to: Mary Wings, 1521 Treat Avenue, San Francisco, CA 94110 USA.

[Haworth co-indexing entry note]: "Nobody Ever Asked Me If I Had an Agent." Wings, Mary. Co-published simultaneously in *Journal of Lesbian Studies* (Harrington Park Press, an imprint of The Haworth Press, Inc.) Vol. 4, No. 4, 2000, pp. 159-164; and: *Lesbian Self-Writing: The Embodiment of Experience* (ed: Lynda Hall) Harrington Park Press, an imprint of The Haworth Press, Inc., 2000, pp. 159-164. Single or multiple copies of this article are available for a fee from The Haworth Document Delivery Service [1-800-342-9678, 9:00 a.m. - 5:00 p.m. (EST). E-mail address: getinfo@haworthpressinc.com].

I do not write every day. Months of long work spates are broken by seasons when I am doing carpentry or painting, the daily chores.

I have no manuscripts hidden in drawers with piles of rejection letters. I can say quite honestly that I have never had the dream of being published. And yet the single spaced, badly typed half finished manuscript of my first novel *She Came Too Late* was optioned during a pleasure trip to London.

One event and one event only led me to writing, and that is emigration.

In 1979 I happily moved to that most beautiful city, Amsterdam in the Netherlands. I had fallen in love with a Dutch woman in an embarrassingly short amount of time. She was halfway through medical school. I was a visual artist. She wanted me to come live with her. We would reside in Holland. I packed my paintbrushes.

I was determined to learn Dutch (unlike most North Americans). A helpful neighbor practiced with me every morning. People seem to have so much time in Holland; there was the generous welfare system and even in offices the coffee break proliferated. And the coffee was great. However, while I was learning the language, relationships–and my reading of personality–were dependent on body language, tone of voice, etc. The complexities of the Dutch social codes, the high educational level of the Dutch citizenry and the frequent conversational challenges kept me on my toes, if not continuously fearful of sounding stupid or approval seeking. My American friendliness was often greeted with suspicion. 'Why are you being so friendly?' was a question I was asked. I still have no answer, except, 'Why not?'

One night Patty and I attended a dinner party given by a woman who I knew had been active in the Dutch resistance. I happily followed her story with my growing vocabulary. I knew that our hostess Henny and her father helped Jews get out of Holland. Henny's father printed fake passports and she took the photographs with film stolen from the Nazis. They were arrested and Henny's father died in a concentration camp when Henny was still a teenager.

However (as I had heard) Henny refused to collect benefits allocated to those who had been active in the resistance. Others who applied for such benefits were viewed as immodest (this I gleaned from earlier knowledge and reading sneers). On this evening Henny recounted a story of a man who had falsely applied for these benefits, claiming that his experiences during the war had psychologically crippled him. During an examination, to underscore his point this man ate all the fish in the goldfish bowl.

That evening on leaving the party I commented to Patty, that it wouldn't be that hard after all, for a Dutchman to swallow goldfish. The Dutch swallow raw herring with gusto. Patty looked at me strangely. "Henny's story was about her vacation in Africa with Mieke."

That is when I learned about how active my fantasy life could be. Especially, when, language lonely, I would make up a narrative to amuse myself, to be part of a social situation, to laugh when others laughed.

I began writing as a solace. I wrote about all the things I missed from my homeland. Mountains and hills. American friendliness, superficial or not. I wrote about sunsets and clouds racing across the canvas of the bay area skies. About people who had no social security net, who drift without cultural identity, where people jump class boundaries, where money was a ticket, and the freedom to be poor is everywhere. There is the energy of the crazy optimism that I missed, tried to capture, set down on the page.

Patty started her residency and was rarely around. I moved into a communal living situation with five women and two children.

This move seemed to solidify my intentions to remain in Holland, although the relationship with Patty was hitting hard times. Few relationships survive medical residency on either of our continents.

A phone call came from the states. My mother, Betty, had had a stomach-ache, was diagnosed with gall bladder trouble, although–it was suggested–there might be something more serious going on. I got off the plane in time to see her emerge from the operating room. Betty died of cancer, a month after her diagnosis. A previously healthy woman, she was 59. I was 29.

My father did not cope well; sinking into a deep depression, he stopped talking. As I flew back and forth to the U.S., I would pick up mystery novels to pass the endless hours waiting in airports, flying over the polar ice cap.

I consumed these novels. They gave me a sense of solving death; the emphasis was on action. There was no grieving, only anger. And clues. It might not have been reality, but the genre was good medicine. Except for one thing.

Crime novels at this time only featured male heroes who drank and fucked their way through exciting adventures. Women characters were at best stupid, at worst, evil and dutifully kept out of the action.

As I flew back and forth over the ocean, wondering how my mother could die so quickly, I also wondered how these pulpy books got published. I kept turning the pages.

My father started talking. He called me in Holland. "Please come live with me," his voice faltered. "I cannot be alone." I had never heard my father cry. "Your voice–you sound just like Betty–please . . ."

My brother took over the family duty of caring for my father while I stayed in Holland. But the rains would be coming soon to northwest Europe, and there was a lot rolling around in my head. The relationship with Patty was deteriorating. I was deteriorating.

Closer to my commune members, I sat glaze-eyed through evening meals. Rita, Ciska, Betty passed me extra helpings and clucked that I was becoming too thin.

"We're your family now" they reassured me and I tried to believe it was true. In September the weather took its wet course. I feared the long winter nights. Now Rita, Ciska and the kids would get up and bike to work in the dark. The rain was continuous.

I noticed how my enterprising roommates all chose new hobbies for the fall, as if this were the normal course of the season. Rita, at fifty, started taking piano lessons. Ciska started up with horseback riding (at an indoor rink of course). Marjan joined a band, Betty had a knitting group with an old group of friends on Tuesday nights. For the most part the sweaters were terrible.

The Dutch culture promotes this kind of creativity, in songs composed for birthdays and anniversaries. Taking joy in the act of doing, no one was looking at the final product.

I thought I would write a story, in English, wonderful, delightful English. A murder mystery, with a woman as the detective. It would take place in California, with clouds racing across the sky, and my character(self) speeding across Bay bridges solving heinous crimes. Certainly no one asked me (as they would have in the States) "Do you have an agent?"

And so we all embarked on our winter pastimes. I became consumed with entertaining, teasing, foiling, my imaginary reader. Getting lost in research. The writing process was pure joy: a universe in which I was in complete control. My painterly sensibilities and love of architecture found play in description. And strangely enough, the characters I thought I had created took on a life of their own, coming up with their own dialogue.

I spoke to my brother on the phone, telling him about this exciting process of novel writing. I asked him to help me think of a title. The character was late for an appointment, and I had thought of *Came Too Late*. My brother said I needed a subject, as in *She Came Too Late*.

"So what are you going to do with it when it's done?" he asked. His question jerked me back into a reality that seemed so bankrupt. "Are you going to get an *agent*?" His words, echoed over the microwave phone line, from a place that was farther away than the miles could measure.

Spring rolled around. We all went to Ciska's *dressage* exposition, amazed at her prowess as she rode a horse the size of a small European car. Rita and Marjan played duets and we laughed ourselves silly trying on Betty's sweaters.

A friend in publishing read my first fifty pages. I was happy enough with her excitement when she asked, "What happens next?"

Only later did she say, in her professional opinion, that *She Came Too Late* could become a 'cult classic.' It turns out she was right, but that is not where this writer started. I wrote from the heart, I wrote for a sense of discovery, I wrote to entertain an imaginary reader, and to gain a sense of self during cataclysimic changes in my life. Shortly after I finished *She Came Too Late* my father died.

And so the first part of this story ends and the second part of this story begins: How to re-emigrate into your own country? How to write not just one, but two, three, four, seven, novels? How to get beyond the boredom with your life ("if I don't get out of this itty bitty room I'm gonna go out of my mind," etc.)? How to get beyond the business of publishing? How to keep your edge?

I have also written commercially: radio programs, short stories, the occasional articles and screenplays. And yes, I have an agent.

But mostly I want to convey the simple, essential lessons of this writer's journey and give you my advice:

If you can, try to get out of the United States of America.

As an ex-matriot you will become so internally full that your experience will somehow force you into expression. If not, the weather will (do emigrate to a wet, nasty climate). You can live dirt cheap, and yes, you can live underground. It keeps you honest.

The practice of language, the telling of your own story, can banish loneliness. Longing will give your writing honesty and edge.

The friction between cultures will make you observant, a bit paranoid and wiser. The act of emigrating will throw you back upon yourself in a way that can be startlingly authentic. And getting out of the American debtor way of life will give you the time to discover your talents.

And if anyone asks you, "Do you have an agent?" then you know you are in the wrong country.

Index

A/k/a 128
Abuse 4,12,15,15-16,27,30,84,94,
    103,109,111,112,136
Absence, absent 10,56,57,144,145,148
Adolescence 33,44,65,74,83,89,135
The Aerial Letter (Brossard) 38
Age, ageism, aging 4,15,17,
    99-100,147
Agency (through writing) 7,8,9,12,
    82,112
AIDS 81,115,118,119-120
Alcohol, alcoholism 27,30,32,49,56,
    66,84,137-138,161
Alien, alienated 74,76,85
Allen, Paula Gunn 33
Allison, Dorothy 84
Amadeus (film) 131
Ameliorate, ameliorography 12,82,111
Anger 30,31,38,64,85,90,99,110,
    145,161
Another Mother (Robson) 125,128
Anxiety (O'Hara) 49
Anzaldúa, Gloria 4,10-11,13,14
Art, artists 28,37,64,105,107,121,
    131,137,153,160
Artificial insemination 91
Astaire, Fred 46
Auden, W.H. 131
Audience 10,55,68,76,80,85,96,116
Autobiography 3,4,5,9,12,27,30,39,40,
    50,82,83,84,133
Autography 9,10,79
Automythology 69

Babies 43, 91-96
Bal, Mieke 70
Baldwin, James 33,74
The Basement (Millett) 101
The Bat Had Blue Eyes (Warland) 145

Beauty 7,22,25,30,34,41,52,53,
    88-89,96,104,110,137,160
  language 6
Bersianik, Louky 100
Biomythography 71
Birth 3,4,27,31,63,87,89,92,94,
    95,96,133,135,144,148
Bisexual 85
Black 61,64,68,70,71,72,75,76,
    77,85,86
  Movement 75,77
Blais, Marie-Claire 100
Bloodroot (Warland) 145
Body
  as text-to-be-read 13,14,18,99,100,
    130,136
  has memory, knowledge 1,13,14,
    130,154
  lesbian 97,98,99,145
  physical 1-5,7,10-15,17-18,24,
    25-27,34,37-39,42-47,52,53,
    55,56,62,65-67,74,76,77,
    82-83,87,91-94,97-100,121,
    127,131,136-138,143,
    151-152,154
  sexual 7,31,65,98,127,130,136,145
  write the body 11,15,57,97,130,
    136,143,154
Body language 7,13,160
Body politic 11,55
Bornstein, Kate 7
Boundaries, borders 10,13,14,18,48,
    51,97,100,110,137
Boundary-crossings 3,8,18,97,100,
    110,161
Brant, Beth 3,5,9,10,11,12,13,15,
    17,21-34
Brossard, Nicole 1,3,8,9,14,16,18,
    35-40,100,148

48,49,50,53,54,57,60,65,67,
85,99,100,109,111,128,130,
142,143,145,154
punctuation 61,65,143
use of dictionaries, thesauri 32,56
Writing as Witness (Brant) 10,21
*Writing from the Heart. Inspiration
and Exercises for Women
Who Want to Write*
(Newman) 62
*Writing for Your Life: A Guide and
Companion to the Inner
Worlds* (Metzger) 62

*Writing Selves: Contemporary
Feminist Autography*
(Perreault) 9
Wyeth, Andrew 52

Xena, Warrior Princess (myth) 73

Yeats, W.B. 131

Zami (Lorde) 72-73

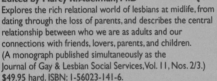